WHAT DARKNESS WAS

THE
SEAGULL
LIBRARY OF
GERMAN
LITERATURE

WHAT DARKNESS WAS

Inka Parei

TRANSLATED BY KATY DERBYSHIRE

LONDON NEW YORK CALCUTTA

GOETHE
INSTITUT

This publication was supported by a grant
from the Goethe-Institut India

Seagull Books, 2021

Originally published as *Was Dunkelheit war by* Inka Parei
© Schöffling & Co. Verlagsbuchhandlung GmbH,
Frankfurt am Main 2005

First published in English translation by Seagull Books, 2013
English translation © Katy Derbyshire, 2013

ISBN   978 0 8574 2 832 5

British Library Cataloguing-in-Publication Data
A catalogue record for this book is available
from the British Library

Typeset in Cochin by Seagull Books, Calcutta, India
Printed and bound by WordsWorth India, New Delhi, India

NOTE FROM THE TRANSLATOR

While Inka Parei's debut, *The Shadow-Boxing Woman*, looked at the effects of German reunification, her second novel, *What Darkness Was*, revolves round two key points in German history: the Second World War and the 'German Autumn' of 1977. Set in a suburb of Frankfurt in September 1977, the book presents a picture of West Germany on the brink of hysteria.

Since the late 1960s, students and other protesters had been rebelling against the strict corset of post-War morals. Aside from the prominent War criminals tried at Nuremberg, many former Nazis had been silently assimilated into a largely conservative society, and young people now began to question and challenge their parents' generation. The journalist Beate Klarsfeld famously slapped Federal Chancellor and former Nazi Kiesinger during a Christian Democratic Party conference at the height of the 1968 protests.

Just as elsewhere, political protests about the Vietnam War, the Arab-Israeli conflict, abortion rights and other issues were accompanied by social experimentation. Communes were set up in an attempt to revolutionize private relations. The burgeoning feminist movement came up with new forms of anti-authoritarian childcare, often referred to as *Kinderläden* or 'children's shops' because they took over vacant shops. Psychiatric patients, apprentices, young people in care homes rebelled against authority and founded their own collectives.

During the early 1970s, a small number of left-wing activists turned their backs on legal forms of protest and looked to terrorism as a strategy to effect change in West German society. The most high profile of these organizations was the Baader-Meinhof group, which eventually called itself the Red Army Faction. After a series of bombings, shootings and bank robberies, by the autumn of 1977 the movement's founders had been arrested and were held under strict conditions at Stammheim prison. A new generation of activists now planned to force their release by terrorist means.

The events of September and October 1977 are known as the 'German Autumn'. On 5 September 1977 a 'commando' kidnapped Hanns Martin Schleyer, a former SS man who had the highly symbolic role of head of the Federation of German Industries and the Confederation of German Employers' Associations.

In his seminal account *Baader-Meinhof. The Inside Story of the RAF* (translated by Anthea Bell), journalist Stefan Aust describes the events:

At about 5.25 p.m., the convoy was driving west down Friedrich-Schmidt-Strasse, which passes Raschdorffstrasse, where Schleyer lived, on the right. Raschdorffstrasse was a one-way street. The two cars had to make a detour to reach Schleyer's apartment.

'There they are,' said Sieglinde Hofmann. [Peter-Jürgen] Boock took his gun out of the pram and hid it under his jacket. Sieglinde Hofmann pushed the pram a little further. The trap was set.

Directly after turning into Vincenz-Statz-Strasse, which runs parallel to Raschdorffstrasse, Schleyer's driver suddenly had to stamp on the brakes. There was a blue pram standing in the road in front of him, and beside it, parked half on the pavement, a yellow Mercedes with Cologne number plates. The car with the three policemen in it ran into the back of Schleyer's car.

As the two cars collided the shooting began. The commando moved in with all guns blazing. [. . .] Boock himself thought that no one could have survived the shoot-out, and went back to fetch the VW minibus. As he reversed it the sliding door, which was not locked, sprang open, and Boock could see Willy Peter Stoll and another member of the group dragging Schleyer out of his car. The others jumped into the bus as well and forced the president of the Employers' Association down on the floor. Stoll had flung himself into the passenger seat beside Boock: 'Come on, get moving!'

The three police guards accompanying Schleyer and his driver were all killed. The kidnappers demanded the release of eleven RAF prisoners, who were to be flown out to a safe country. After weeks of investigations, negotiations and government delaying tactics, the terrorists tried to step up the pressure on the West German cabinet through the hijacking of the Lufthansa plane *Landshut* during a flight from Palma de Mallorca to Frankfurt. In the early hours of 18 October the German elite police unit GSG9 stormed the plane, now in Mogadishu, shooting the four Arab hijackers and releasing all the hostages unharmed. The next morning, the RAF prisoners Andreas Baader and Gudrun Ensslin were found dead in their cells; Jan-Carl Raspe died of gunshot wounds later that day and Irmgard Möller was operated on for stab wounds to her chest. Despite numerous conspiracy theories, Aust concludes that they had committed suicide. Hanns Martin Schleyer was killed by his kidnappers the next day.

Inka Parei was ten years old in 1977 and living in the building she describes so precisely in *What Darkness Was*. Her father ran the ground-floor *Gaststätte*—something between a public house and a licensed restaurant. She remembers those tense weeks as a very dramatic time, a state of emergency with 'wanted' posters at every bus stop. The author had an unusual perspective—as her parents were busy running the pub, she spent most afternoons there after school, eating lunch and helping out, listening in on guests' conversations without being part of them, as if they were being staged for her in the pub, a place on the boundary between public and private space.

The 'German Autumn', she told me, polarized West German society. There were those who supported the terrorists' aims, and those who demanded an even tougher government reaction. Everyone seemed to feel responsible in some way—what would you do if they knocked at your door? What would you do if it was your wife wielding the machine gun? What would you do if you were running the government? These were concerns among the regulars in that Frankfurt pub in 1977.

The questions posed by the rebellious generation of 1968 were Inka Parei's questions too. Her father was born in 1921 and had been a soldier in the Wehrmacht. She remembers all the stories about the War, related in the pub and at home, the same scenes over and over. And she remembers the gaps in those narratives, the things that were never said.

It was not until the controversial 'Wehrmacht Exhibition' in the late 1990s that German society began to admit that ordinary soldiers had been extensively and systematically involved in War crimes, rather than pinning the blame entirely on the SS. Wehrmacht soldiers, as the exhibition showed, were actively involved in the Holocaust, in looting occupied territories particularly in eastern Europe, in the mass murder of civilians and in the appalling treatment of Soviet prisoners of War. Objections to the exhibition raised its profile further, prompting public debate at long last.

It was in this context that Inka Parei went back to Frankfurt to revisit the house where she grew up. The rooms were the same, only the furnishings had changed. *What Darkness Was*, Inka told me, is a narrative experiment, an attempt to simulate an entire generation—that of her father—through a single individual. She was seeking a connection between a private context and the public debate. Her unnamed protagonist, an old man on his deathbed, is enclosed within his constricted home but has a view of the world from his window and finds himself drawn into public events large and small just as he finally remembers his own past. The events of 1977 trigger a very slow recourse to his suppressed memories, almost mirroring the experience of the nation as a whole.

Inka Parei writes with a clean precision that tallies perfectly with her subject matter. Translating her is a challenge and a joy, as she opens my eyes to tiny details and major historical contexts. I am certain that this book will appeal to the readers in the same way.

Berlin

March 2012

What Darkness Was

The building was on the western edge of Frankfurt near a river, the Nidda. The old man had not expected to inherit it; he had been shocked when he found out. To begin with, he hadn't been able to recall its former owner.

It had a post-War facade, grubby and expressionless. It probably hadn't been painted since the end of the fifties. The plaster on the front wall consisted of rough, worm-shaped notches, in which the dirt of past decades had gathered and formed black grooves. It was a corner building with a public house and a butcher's shop on the ground floor; and the street on which it stood, Alt-Rödelheim, was narrow and winding. By day, a very noisy tram trundled past it at ten-minute intervals, labelled '23 Röderbergweg'. He liked the noise; it soon felt familiar and the nights' silence seemed artificial.

Like many people who moved house at his age, he had not really got used to his new surroundings; part of him was still living in Berlin. When he was tired or if he'd had one or two drinks too many, he occasionally failed to find his bed straight away, or he caught himself looking for the doors on the wrong side of the rooms.

He hadn't wanted to take much with him when he moved. He had left behind his living-room shelves and given his books to a neighbour, who sold bric-a-brac on a vacant lot near Möckern Bridge in Kreuzberg on the weekends. The dealer had showed him the long wooden crates in which the belongings of the deceased were sold off, their letters and family photos and personal documents, and as a result he had burnt the remaining photos he owned.

His new living room housed just two armchairs and a table and an old glass-fronted cabinet. The table was usually bare but for a colourless tablecloth and a tropical-wood box meant for visitors, containing ancient cigarettes.

By the time he woke up on the evening of that sixth of September, it was dark. He had dozed off at the window, his ear pressing up against the glass. He jumped and rubbed the cooled-off side of his face. It was night outside but he hadn't seen the darkness coming, nor the rain. The rain made no sound at all.

For a moment he was not sure where he was. He had had a bad dream. The windowpane in front of him was clouded over, everything behind it blurred, with no depth of perception. He wiped his shirtsleeve across the glass. Below him was a thick curve of asphalt, changing colour soundlessly, twisting round the buildings like an animal's spine and ending a few yards on in a driveway. He saw parked cars and, slightly further off, the light of a streetlamp, glittering dull and coarse-grained on the damp patches of the cobbles. The facade of the building opposite was only a few steps away. It leant forwards, a wall of slates layered over one another like reptilian scales.

He had forgotten what the dream had been about; all he knew was that it had been cold. There had been a smell of snow and he had seen birch trunks. He had been seeing them often recently — closely planted birch trees bearing traces of bullet marks.

All he listened to for a few minutes was his breathing. It was a moonless night, turned cool. The pub landlord's children were wailing. Their bedroom light was still on. The noise came up to him very loudly; the backyard, which he had begun looking out on more and more often, by day and night, was like a shaft that collected sounds, even the slightest whisper.

He took out his binoculars from behind the radiator and trained them on the opposite wall.

He had never owned anything big, not even a car. Of course, he had much more money coming in now than before but the income did not mean much to him. He had spent nights poring over the papers they had handed over to him, his mind particularly occupied by the insurance policies on the building. He had read through all the regulations connected to them but had been forced to admit that he did not understand all of them. He didn't know which catastrophes the building was really protected against; he was always alert now.

Above the parking spaces was the flat rented to a family called the Dörrs. They were the oldest tenants in the building. They overheated their flat even in summer, condensation dripping from the kitchen windows. The wife was sitting at the kitchen table with her knitting; he saw part of her legs and a plastic bowl full of balls of wool. The Dörrs' son was standing next to her by the cooker, a pimply youth with a moustache. He stirred something in a saucepan and launched an empty tin at the rubbish bin without looking.

The younger children's bedroom was one floor up, usually untidy; he thought it looked sordid. The wardrobe doors were open and a swaying lamp cast a dull light across the room, fractured by threads of raffia.

They were girls. He didn't understand why they never wore nightgowns. They were sitting on the top bunk, a tangle of mangy arms and legs in towelling pyjamas. He couldn't tell at first glance whether they were fighting or protecting one another but then he saw that they were arguing. Their hair was tousled and the older girl was pressing her shoulder into her younger sister's belly, while she in turn clasped her hands round her neck from behind.

When the girls saw someone coming they drew apart and both began shouting. A man's hand came into view, a fist enclosing two toothbrushes. The heads of the brushes poked out at the top. The pub landlord was a bulky, black-haired man in his mid-fifties with remarkably large bags under his eyes. He pointed at objects lying around in the room and yelled something and then he walked up to the bunk beds and unfastened his belt buckle.

The old man lowered his binoculars, his hands trembling. He had rough, sturdy hands covered in age spots and white patches devoid of pigment, the veins raised visibly beneath the skin. He had the furrowed hands of a man who does physical work even though he had never really done hard labour; he'd worked at the post office.

He could almost hear the hissing sound the leather of the belt made as it slid out of the loops. The younger of the two girls risked a glance outside, which suddenly grew long, hesitant, as if she had seen him. Then she turned away and ran to the door and someone extinguished the light.

Something unpleasantly loud made him jump not much later. He got a shock; he must have dozed off again. He did not like the noise; he felt cold.

It's the insomnia, he thought. It makes me feel dazed.

Absent-mindedly, he lifted his head from the glass and scratched at his chin. His other hand, which had just been prone on his lap, stroked restlessly across his legs, coming across a crumpled handkerchief, and wandered on from there to his left knee. He felt it carefully and forced his hand into the gap between the wall and the radiator, a little way, and from there he felt his way up and across the windowsill.

It was bare.

He wondered what time it might be. In the giddiness of awakening he had lost his feeling for time, which confused him; he always knew exactly what time it was.

He turned round with care. The remains of his evening meal were still on the table: a half-eaten slice of bread spread with liverwurst, a gherkin. There it was again — that strange noise. Someone seemed to be shaking the door of the hotel below him.

He leant forwards and looked down. The backyard was still and cold. Everything was dark opposite; the windows in the other part of the building were closed up with brown shutters at night. They looked small and blind, like mediaeval crenels. On one side of the house was the butcher's vegetable patch, covered the day before with a tarpaulin from a delivery van emblazoned with a pig. A fork protruded from the pig's back, its body was divided up and numbered into the sections for use after slaughtering, and spaces gaped between its thighs and body, like missing joints. A layer of water had formed on the surface of the tarpaulin, seeping into the grooves of a crookedly paved path with crumbling edges, which led from the bed to a washing line and from there to the entrance to the building. A child's length of elastic dangled from a post, underneath it a tin pail, a shell-shaped sieve poking out of it, small, gnawed balls and spade handles.

The hotel belonged to the pub, one corridor with five or six rooms coming off it, most of them on the other side facing the next-door building. The corridor was linked to the stairwell by a fire door but the door was never used. He very rarely heard any sound from the hotel guests, although he suspected that two of the rooms bordered on his own walls—the one in his bedroom and the wall in the kitchen.

The rain had set in more strongly now, falling in thick, diagonal lines. It had not rained for a long time. The summer had been hot and muggy and the sky almost always pale blue in a hazy, smudgy way. A very diluted cloud layer had hung in the sky for weeks without raining but now the water was dripping out of the gutter pipes and pooling in the drains. The concrete channels dissected the yard into three parts, meeting in the middle in a hollow, an ancient sewer entry. A grating choked with limestone and sealing flax covered it, exuding the scent of decay, with broken bars that had rusted back together crookedly, brown and cracked. After strong rain the yard flooded, stinking of rubbish for days.

The old man tugged his tank top over his hips. The rattling downstairs was not stopping—an unsettling, urgent sound—and now there was knocking as well. He looked down at his legs. They thickened in the wrong places, not where the muscles ought to be, which made them look perfectly straight and pliable in a limp way, like the limbs of stuffed toys.

He straightened up. He was always slightly dizzy when he stood up after a long time, and for a moment he felt as if he consisted solely of his legs. He waited for the dizziness to pass and then picked up his crutches, grey poles ending in three rubber feet. He felt his way slowly forwards, as he always did to begin with or on slippery ground or when he felt unsure of himself. He leant on the right crutch and pushed his foot forwards slightly and then the left crutch, until his legs and his crutches were positioned diagonally to one another like four limbs, and made his way along the hall to the kitchen.

The hall seemed dark and narrow as a ditch. The walls were painted in a shade that must have been there forever, a gloomy yellow or green over remnants of wallpaper, only attached by the layer of paint. There was a damp, metallic smell. The shaking was less clearly audible now.

He stopped at the kitchen doorway. His kitchen was small, an untiled room with a top-hinged window between two slopes of the roof. When he stood all the way in the room he filled it almost entirely and could only turn to all sides with cautious quarter-turns, to the cooker, to the dresser and to the table. He switched on the light, inched forwards and tugged at the drawer under the tabletop. It emerged, smelling rather sharply of grease, lined with paper and containing a jumble of pencil stubs, crumpled coupons, old ballpoint pens, corks and red and green rubber bands. Among them were his tenants' keys: access to the Dörrs' flat, garage and cellar, labelled and held together by a loop of tape, a ring on a brown-leather fob that the pub landlord had recently given him and another pair, the keys to the front and back doors of the butcher's shop. The butcher had bought the rear part of the building from him at the very beginning and demolished it, then built himself a new home, a low, ugly building with a sauna in the basement. All the keys to the house that the old man possessed were tied together with parcel string into a large, jangling, interconnected whole, apart from one that he had never used—a flat, brass-coloured key. He took it out and put it in his pocket.

Someone ought to wake up, he thought. The landlord and his wife ought to have woken up by now.

They were probably too tired. They were woken every morning by machinery and the shouts of the road-menders. Their bedroom was at the front of the building

above the centre of a building site, where workers had
been ripping up parts of old pavements for days and
piling them onto vans, from six thirty in the morning to
three in the afternoon, in carefully marked rows like
bones excavated at a dig. Too little sleep was like a blanket that was too thin or too short, something you could
not help tugging at, in a constantly restless and alert
state. In this kind of sleep, any disruptive sounds that
did not indicate immediate danger were shaken off with
uneasy movements that insinuated them into dreams. It
was a cold sleep. You never got warm, you shivered on
awakening. He imagined the two of them, the pub landlord and landlady, pale, hung-over and thirsty, pulling
their blankets over their faces, tossing to and fro to ban-
ish the knocking outside.

It's just the same with me, he thought. It was the
first time the connection occurred to him. I'm always
freezing and I sleep that thin, dreary sleep like in my
time as a soldier, except I'm not tired at all any more, at
least not when I try to close my eyes. Never at all.

He turned round to the niche behind the kitchen
door where his crutches stood. One of them tipped over
and fell on a pile of old newspapers. He leant over to
pick it up and gazed at the face of Elvis Presley. It was
a picture from not long before his death, a close-up. He
could make out the droplets of sweat on his neck, the
dark shadows under his eyes and every one of his hairs,
lit up by a stage light from behind and looking grey in a
strange way, drained of colour.

It was dark in the stairwell. The corridor smelt of cleaning fluids. The rubber feet of his crutches always adhered very firmly to the black stone floor; they made a slurping sound when he lifted them as he walked. The old man laid his hand on the light switch. Behind him, he felt the draught from the open window in the living room, then it slammed shut and with it the door, and almost at the same time a cellar lock slammed, down in the belly of the house. He leant against the wall, rubbing his head on its cool surface for a moment. Then he thought of something. He felt for his keys in the front pocket of his trousers but even as he did so he knew he had the keys with him. They had been on the hook above the stove as usual; he had removed them with his usual hand movement before he left the kitchen. Recently, he had begun to guard pedantically over his keys and papers, drawn curtains and smoothed table-cloths, and as he stood against the wall now, breathless and slightly confused, it seemed to him as if he was step-ping out of this habit with the hurried exit from his front door, like stepping out of a picture. As a young man he had been very absent-minded and forgetful, he knew that all too well. He just rarely thought back to it.

The fire door was right next to the banisters. He took a few steps up to the rail, leant his crutches against it and fetched the key. The stairwell light reflected in the paint on the door, dazzling him for an instant. The door was painted white, even the handle and the lock con-cealed behind a plastic disc. He pressed the handle down and tried to push the disc aside but it was stuck fast, glued to the rest of the door by the paint. He scratched at it with the edge of the key and the binding gave way.

The key fit. He pushed the door open and reeled back slightly as an unpleasant, stuffy warmth welled up towards him. He was compelled to cough and as the coughing lurched his torso forwards he almost stumbled over the metal threshold separating the two corridors from one another. He let out a quiet curse and held onto the doorframe, then entered the hotel corridor.

The hallway was narrow with a low ceiling; it smelt of nicotine. On one side of the corridor were the doors to the guest rooms; opposite them was the long ledge of a radiator cover, dotted with earthenware jugs and beer mugs and a couple of empty leaflet holders from the tourist-information office. He couldn't remember when he had last been here — it must have been some time ago. At the other end, a short staircase led downward. He stopped once he had reached it. The crutches got in his way on stairs so he had to tie them together with the fabric tabs on one of the handles to hang them over his shoulders, and then, he thought, he would take a tight grip on the banisters with both hands so that he could push his legs slowly along the steps, one after another. But now he realized that the shaking had stopped and there was not a sound of knocking in the house either, and he stopped still for a moment, as if numbed by this realization and uncertain which direction to take now. He yawned and slouched slightly. He was getting cold again. Someone in the building pulled a toilet flush and a car tyre screeched in the distance.

I should have lain down, thought the old man, instead of stumbling around here in the middle of the night. I'm a stubborn old mule; I'm so exhausted. I might have been able to have a proper, deep sleep for once.

It took him a moment to notice the stranger. The old man was standing on the second step, lost in thought and annoyed at himself, and looking distractedly down at where the end of the stairs vanished into the darkness of a small reception room. A few patches of light from the lamp in the yard fell through the door. There was a zinc pail against one wall, next to it a scrubbing brush. A cleaning cloth had been spread out over the pail and had dried into shape draped over the edge. Someone had knocked it off and now it lay inverted, pointlessly mimicking the opening of the bucket, on the doormat.

He saw the tips of two shoes and knees swathed in grey flannel, and it was not until then that he recognized the rest, the whole of the man sitting against the wall with his legs drawn up, apparently unconscious or asleep.

The headlights of a car leaving the yard shone through the door and lit up the reception room, which confused him. He tried to understand what was going on but he didn't quite manage, not as quickly as he ought to have done. He knew the entire situation would now proceed without him taking any action; he was simply in the middle of it, defenceless, in a strange stairway. It was a brief moment of descending panic until he realized that there was absolutely no connection between the figure in the hotel lobby and the headlights. They were probably from the butcher's van, driving to the meat market as he did several nights a week. There was a pergola against the back wall of the new house, cutting the yard off to the south, he remembered, with a climber growing on it. It was definitely the headlights of the butcher's van casting their light into the entrance, one shining brightly and the other, semicovered by the leaves, duller and patchier. He saw the outline of a fire extinguisher as the ray of light moved slowly across the lobby, and two glittering dots: eyes.

I've locked myself in, called the stranger.

He had a loud, deeply booming voice. His legs opened up and the old man saw something flashing, something dangling from a ring and a chain that the other man was looping round one of his fingers with a twisting motion. He felt his heart beat more loudly as the chain flashed briefly in the light, remembering the fascination that circular movements had exerted on him as a child, the moment in which an object seemed gradually to dissolve through increasing speed, although in reality it was only his eyes that couldn't keep up with the motion. Then the delivery van rounded the corner, a pile of empty meat troughs scraping across the load bed and the urging sound of the engine, revved up into the next gear, echoed on one of the empty, wet streets on the other side of the row of houses. It was a sound that always scared him, for some inexplicable reason.

The lobby was now bathed in darkness again except for a cone of light near the doormat, and the banister, which slanted beneath his hand like a downhill road, disappeared into the black a few yards below him. He wondered why the stranger hadn't called loudly from the very beginning. A voice that loud would easily have been heard; he needn't have broken the lock. Something about it seemed typical for the young people he often came across. He wondered what it was—perhaps a certain fixation with dealing with objects in situations that were really about people.

Can you hear me? called the stranger. I can't get out.

There was a hint of panic in his voice, only a brief fluctuation, a flutter in his pitch, but the old man was unsettled; he was not certain any more whether he hadn't been so immersed in his thoughts for a moment that he hadn't heard the man at all.

The stranger held up his keys. One of them had broken off at the shaft. He jumped up and switched on the light. A windowless room with a reception counter came into view, with a handbell and an empty home-made key box on a dusty glass sheet behind the desk.

You ought to have that lock seen to, the man continued. It sticks, you can see that. He came up the stairs,
taking two at a time.

He stopped directly below the old man and they
looked one another in the eye. The old man was startled,
though he did not know why. The stranger had long,
very muscular arms that made his suit look slightly too
short. His jacket was open, a shirt made of thin white
material peeking out, and chest hair was visible between
his skin and the cloth, like tiny protruding shadows.

I'm sorry, he said, seeming to realize now that he
was not dealing with a hotel employee. I must have
woken you but I have to go back out to the car park, I've
got something to unload.

There's another exit, the old man said quietly.

He brushed against the other man's body with his
head lowered, raising himself back onto the landing with
great concentration. He felt some kind of moisture
exuding from the man; he couldn't make out whether it
was sweat or rain but he sensed the air growing cooler
in his immediate vicinity and the greasy smell of damp
woollen fabric. Above the man's right ankle there was a
strange, elongated lump where the seam of his trousers
had slipped upwards.

Wait a moment, said the stranger. Let me hold the
door open for you.

He squeezed carefully past him and walked a couple of steps ahead. Then he realized it would take the old

man a while to reach the end of the corridor, and he stood there undecidedly for a moment until he remembered the room he'd rented. It really looked as if he'd forgotten it up to that moment. His eyes briefly searched the row of doors and then he went to one of the middle rooms, put his hand on the door handle and disappeared inside. The room had not been locked.

The old man stopped walking. It was very quiet in the house now—the kind of quiet that only existed in the early hours of the morning, when the streets were empty and most people were still asleep. It was a silence in which you could feel the absence of sound in all the lifeless things that cities consist of, the silence of the mortar, the walls and rails, the aluminium casings, the silence of the wood and the hewn stones. It was quite different to the countryside, where it's not much quieter at night than in the daytime, and he loved that. In the early hours of the morning he stood awake among motionless things, in the entire labyrinth that the city became without its people, and he knew that wind and light and water were settling upon it but that they all meant nothing.

For a while all he listened to was the scraping of his feet and the crunching sound his sticks made when he released his pressure on them to lift them and put them down again at a different point further along. Then he heard a dragging noise. It sounded like heavy boxes or cartons being pulled out from under a bed and heaved up. He reached the middle of the corridor. The stranger appeared in the doorframe, gave a weak smile and closed the door behind him. The room had only been visible for a moment—a narrow rectangle, pale-brown wallpaper with stalks stuck onto it, straw fibres or at least an imitation and a flimsy wardrobe that looked wobbly, more like a chest. But no cartons; perhaps he'd only imagined the cartons. They didn't speak again. The stranger slipped through the exit and held the steel door open for him. He looked away as he climbed over the raised threshold. The two of them walked the few steps to his front door slowly side by side and he noticed the stranger was breathing quickly, though he hadn't seen him jumping or running. When they got there he pointed at the second staircase, at the bottom of which was another exit that was not usually locked. They parted with no words of goodbye.

The old man knew it would only be a few hours before daybreak was visible through the landing window. Sometimes he stood out here if he hadn't found peace during the night. It was not yet light that shone in then, he could just see that a slightly greater brightness emanated from the shapes outside, in that very moment when the beginning of sunrise wafted its questioning, urging dark blue into the air, while inside the house it was still night for a little longer. He suddenly longed for the brightness of daybreak; he would come back here at the right time, he promised himself, and look out of this small window from which he could see outside as if looking into another time. Whether it was the future or the past didn't matter at those moments.

He closed his front door, held the key clutched tight in his fist and leant against the wall. His sciatic nerve twitched. Just stand here, he thought, just press your feet firmly into the carpet. He had the feeling of offering his body the motionlessness as if in an exchange, in which one partner musters the other closely and persistently and tries not to do anything wrong that might spoil the deal.

But it was impossible not to move at all; some muscle or other was always moving. He suppressed a yawn and the pain kicked in. It felt as if a very large area had suddenly gone up in flames. A while ago he had seen a fire on an oilrig in the Atlantic. The flames had covered half a square kilometre of the water surface almost without transition, a blazing, wind-blown coat of fur atop the waves. He touched his face; it was wet with sweat. He rubbed the moisture off across his cheeks and felt salt running into the tiny cracks in his lips, and then he fell. One of the sticks fell onto his back; he pushed it away and crept a tiny way forwards across the carpet.

He had a good memory. Not for names but for faces. He memorized a person's features like writing. He knew he had seen the face of the man in the corridor once before, not long ago — it must have been yesterday. Or the day before? No, it was yesterday. He was hot now and he was agitated, trying to remember the past day, staring through the silence and the dust he had stirred up just above the floor, staring at a point on the other side of the wall, on the other side of his bedroom door, but it was no use. He had seen the man, that was all he knew now, and it couldn't have been from close up because of his eyes—he would definitely have remembered them. As they stood close to one another in the hallway, he had seen that the man had brown flecks in his eyes. Blue eyes, and the speckles in them had looked like some kind of fluid that had accidentally found its way in and then frozen, as though they affected his sight, but he knew that was an illusion. In reality it was him, looking at the stranger, who was distracted by eyes like that, plunged into confusion and overlooking other things.

He was lying face-down now, flat on the carpet like on a raft, with another five feet to his bedroom. He decided to make an attempt to propel himself forwards as if paddling, by pulling the edge of the carpet towards him. If I can drag myself hand over hand to the bedroom door, he thought, then from there I might be able to reach the edge of the bed with my arms outstretched. He tried to keep his torso stiff and only move his hands and upper arms.

Ten minutes later he was in the bedroom doorway, lying with his head on the floorboards and smelling the dust and the old grey floorboard paint and something acrid. He remembered he hadn't made it to the toilet in time a few days ago. He clutched hold of the bedpost and pulled but the front of his waistband caught on the threshold and the rear part pressed unpleasantly into his lower vertebrae. He let go of the post, undid his pyjama button, grabbed the front of his trousers and pushed it across the edge. Now he heard footsteps outside his front door, hesitating in between and accompanied by a scraping, which sounded as if the stranger was dragging something after him, something too heavy to carry. He waited until the noises died down and tried again to force his body over the threshold, and this time he managed it, reaching the bed frame and pulling himself up.

He had made a resolution to look up at the sky as he was dying.

It was a few days ago that he had first felt a kind of restlessness. It had suddenly bothered him that he always stared at the same spot as he fell asleep and woke up, at the unfamiliar ceiling, at the grubby lampshade and the cobwebs hanging from it. They trembled when the window was open at the top, and sometimes an old fruit fly or the desiccated body of a mosquito came loose and fell onto his bedcover. The woman from the welfare people in Bockenheim who came once a month had moved his bed slightly, into an alcove between the window and the washbasin, and now, lying down, he could look outside whenever he liked. When the time came, he sometimes imagined, he would be able to see the middle of the sky, a deep blue that was neither near nor far away.

For a while he lay motionless on top of the cover, on his side, slightly bent, his trousers undone.

It was cool in the room.

He thought back to the time when he'd lived in Potsdam as a young lad. Back then he had always wanted to ride a horse. Not later though. After the War he had avoided the sight of horses. He'd had two friends: a thin, blond boy called Heiner and another one whose name he couldn't remember any more. They used to go boating along the lakes and rivers in Brandenburg. Sometimes they'd been away for days at a time, sharing a tiny, grey tent at night. When they were too lazy to row they'd doze on the water, floating along half-naked for hours. The names of the lakes they had passed through occurred to him; he spoke them out loud and he felt himself trembling. And he felt the dazzle of the light reflecting off the water behind the closed eyelids of the person he'd been as a boy, and the warmth that enclosed him like an extra skin when he'd laid in the sun for too long.

Perhaps I'm in luck, he thought. Perhaps I've still got a rheumatic plaster somewhere.

He felt for the objects on his bedside table. His arm accidentally brushed against his clock, a travel alarm clock, and it fell over and disappeared into the metal case it had been propped up in with a loud flapping noise. He felt a bottle of rubbing alcohol, a pair of scissors, a fever thermometer and the elastic support he

sometimes wore round his knee when the pain got too
strong. The cup next to it contained semi-evaporated
tea, giving off a strange smell.

He didn't like looking for things. It wasn't the feeling of not having something at hand which he needed
urgently that bothered him but the idea that at the same
moment other things that belonged to him might not be
in the places he had chosen for them, and that they
might reveal something about him in his absence, like
circumstantial evidence.

There was something on the floor. He fished for it —
the plaster. He tore open the wrapper, turned on his side
and pressed it against his lower vertebrae. A viscid,
tingly warmth spread across his back. For the length of
a few breaths he savoured the thrust of heat, and then he
pulled his trousers down and reached for the bedcover.
Once he was done he sighed with relief.

He thought of the fire door again. As far as he could
remember there hadn't been any mechanism to fix the
door in place, so if the stranger hadn't pressed the handle
down properly it was probably still slightly ajar. A large
enough gap to make it rattle in a draught though, and he
didn't like that thought. It wrestled with him, against the
sleep he now willed to come. He had made an effort earlier not to look at the place where the paint had come off
as he opened the lock; it had unsettled him that he could
see across the layers of different coats of paint as if looking back across decades, down to the surface.

I don't want to look down to the surface, he thought. I'll have to get it seen to.

The next time he came to, the room was still dark.

His eyes fell on the perpetual calendar on the washing basket opposite him—a gift from his former employers, the Berlin-Wedding Post Office, for his twenty-fifth year of service. He usually set the small tabs with numbers on them before he went to bed; when he woke up the new date was already looking him in the eye. He liked that but this time it was not the case; the old date was still there.

The stranger came to mind again. He tried to remember where he had seen him before. He knew it was important but his memory only unearthed fragments, sharply focused objects floating through a slate-grey void like remnants of a dream. He saw shattered glass, blond hair, a hand on the railing of a bridge, bloodstains on a wooden post. The wood confused him; by turns it was crooked or splintered, as if cut with a blunt axe, and then slim and straight and suddenly perhaps more of a plank than a trunk, dyed green on one side like the wood used on building sites.

I have to start again from the beginning, he thought. Go through it in order. I know I saw him.

For a while now he'd had problems keeping things he'd experienced recently in mind; he remembered too many details. Times that were further back though, especially the War years and the time before that, were getting clearer and clearer. It often seemed as if he could move directly inside those days, feeling what he had felt back then but at the same time understanding his actions in a way only possible in retrospect—a ghostly clarity that he didn't like.

He wondered when he had woken up, and he still knew: at six thirty. Yesterday was a Tuesday—that was when the beer truck came.

The sun glared that morning. He hadn't closed the curtains and it shone in through the window. The heavy iron slabs slammed in the yard as the men from the brewery opened the hatch to the beer cellar. He heard rattling and someone shouting. He sat up in bed and looked down at the chain that locked the hatch; the padlock fastened to it came loose, falling against the wall and knocking off a lump of plaster.

Watch out, yelled one of the men, a redhead with a beard. You'll be breaking the windows next. He picked up the padlock and inspected the dent in the plaster; a lump of mortar had come loose and dust trickled down onto his shoes. The other man who had thrown the chain, almost a child still, turned away, throwing his head back in defiance. They put down boards to roll the barrels into the hatch. Once they were done the men leant against the wall, took off their gloves and put them in the pockets of their leather aprons. He saw them smoking, tired, blinking into the white of the light with thick eyelids.

Did you hear about Beckenbauer? asked the older man. He extracted a small piece of paper from his shirt pocket and unfolded it several times over, smiling a crooked smile.

Hear what? replied the younger one.

About going to the Cosmos.

What about it?

I know why he's doing it now. It's not for the money at all.

The old man pushed his window open, wanting to get a look. It was a magazine clipping the beer delivery-man was holding up, showing two women arm in arm with a man; he wasn't sure but perhaps it was Franz Beckenbauer. One woman was black and the other white; they were wearing curly wigs and hats draped in the Stars and Stripes. Next to them was an American road cruiser and in the background he made out the wreck of a church tower.

But that's Berlin.

No, you can see they're Yanks.

The redheaded man shrugged and put the photo back in his pocket. The scent of coffee pervaded the yard from the kitchen of the butcher's shop; they smelt it and exchanged glances.

What do they get? asked the younger man. Two lots of Pilsener?

The older man expelled smoke from his nose and yawned. He held his cigarette facing inwards in his hand, his fingers curled round it as if to protect it from a draught. Two lots of Pilsener, three barrels of lager, one crate of bottled beer.

And the empties?

Down there in the corridor.

They threw their stubs on the cobbles and trod them out. The old man saw the younger of them heading for the beer cellar. The older one whistled a tune, taking out his gloves and wiping his head before he disappeared towards the street. There was the sound of him starting the engine and reversing. The back of the truck appeared in the driveway; the hiss of the pneumatic brakes echoed unpleasantly close, as if trapped between the tightly positioned walls.

The driver climbed down from the truck, walked round the back, folded back a tarpaulin and hoisted himself up. Silver-glinting barrels were piled in pyramids on the loading space, alongside towers of crates fastened in place with ropes.

The young lad's head appeared for a moment in the hatch. There was a dull sound of dampened clinking of bottles mixed with the scrape of crates and then he came up the steps again, the other man standing motionless for a while and waiting. The steps to the beer cellar were steep, a spiral staircase. A small, dust-coloured rat came darting out of one of the cracks in the cellar walls across the steps, scurrying over the lad's shoes as he felt his way slowly up. It turned in a few tight, nervous circles and vanished again.

For a while the men unloaded barrels and lined them up at the entrance to the hatch.

When he pushed the window open he saw them sitting down there on the barrels.

Can you imagine your wife ever doing something like that? asked the younger man. He had his elbows propped on his thighs and was gazing at the overflowing rubbish bins next to the back door of the pub.

What? What d'you mean? His partner was balancing a clipboard on his lap, running his pen down a list.

Your wife, in the getaway car, holding a machine gun.

There was silence for a moment. The older man said nothing, only looking up from his clipboard with his eyebrows raised, and then they laughed and went inside past the cellar doorway. He watched them go and then looked down at the beer barrels. They dazzled him when he looked for too long; they were covered in scratches that shone white in the sunlight—frantic, undecipherable handwriting.

Outside, a church bell rang. There was something important, something that had to be kept hold of, but the old man didn't know what it was.

Something always got stuck, on nights like this. A tree, a piece of uniform or now: *a machine gun*. And then he'd see it all day long, as if painted onto a boundless void, whenever he closed his eyes. He saw it like something he had overlooked, something he ought to have got rid of.

Something that protruded in on him from an imaginary margin, the margin of his existence. And this margin had always stayed close to him, all the years, although he had hoped that the long length of his life would take him farther away from it. To a safe centre. To a place where there were lots of people.

He thought about the abduction the deliverymen had been talking about. Yes, he did know about it. There had been wanted posters of terrorists for weeks and they had shown a photo of the victim on the news, a fat man with horn-rimmed glasses. The newsreader had been wearing a black dress—he remembered that because it had seemed unfitting, as if the hostage was already dead.

He tried to sit up. It was difficult.

The pain near his lower vertebrae seemed to have gone but he was sweaty and thirsty and the plaster stuck to his back unpleasantly. He pressed one arm behind himself and ripped it off the skin, his teeth clenched.

His eyes grazed the alarm-clock case on his bedside table; he picked it up and twisted at it, impatient. His hands slipped off—the box was smooth and cold. Inside it the clock rattled when he shook it, which annoyed him. He wanted to know the time, he longed for an end to his holding out in the night, for an end to the dull, reality-contorting mixture of exhaustion and waiting that the night forced upon him. He shook the case again and listened. It went on ticking inside, time proceeding invisibly in there.

The building workers had arrived at seven. He couldn't
see them from his bedroom. He only heard them: their
cars and vans arriving, doors slamming, the jangle of
hammers and pickaxes as they unloaded their tools and
threw them on the pavement, orders yelled into the morning, forceful and bad-tempered. They were installing new
electricity and telephone cables in the road, pulling up
half the pavements. While some of the men were digging
trenches in front of the building, others shovelled them
closed again further along near the bridge. Two workers
spent all day on their knees cobbling the road—a
strange sight, watching them work with their strong
hands between the nylon threads that marked the edges
for the cobbled pattern; they looked like giants behind a
finely woven fence. He had watched them for some
time, enjoying the game of tessellating stones; he
remembered their faces irritated by warmth and hard
work, their bare torsos on which the sun of the past
summer had marked out a landscape of tan, sunburnt
blisters and pale curves in the shape of their vests. But
that had been later. Before that the Meals on Wheels
driver, a Yugoslavian, had brought his lunch. He had
begun giving him a tip so that he'd carry his crutches
downstairs for him. It meant he didn't go outside until
the afternoon but that didn't matter too much. He didn't
get far now anyway. Had he ever got very far?

The question formed soundlessly, like a shock. He
gripped at his chest, stroking it, feeling his chest hairs
down to the roots, an unpleasant sensation.

Before Potsdam he had lived in Berlin. As a child, he had often sat out on the street outside the building where he and his parents lived at the time, a dark, dank tenement building going back a long way from the street, which was demolished later, in the twenties. Whenever he wanted to be on his own, he'd take a small stool and find himself a spot outside. He sat on the wooden stool and stared at his bare feet; it was spring. He thought about his teacher's atlas, which he had been allowed a look at the day before. One particular picture in the middle of the large book, otherwise locked carefully away at the end of class, had stayed in his memory: Europe, physical map. The mountains that had most impressed him were the Urals. He didn't quite know why; perhaps because of the exactness, the precision with which they reared up between the plains.

He opened his mouth. A strange stuffiness seemed to be pervading the room. He groaned, pressed his hand to his ribcage and felt across it, as if to find an opening. But all he felt was the hardness of the bones and a small, familiar indentation, beneath which his heart beat hectically.

Seven thirty.

The landlord's wife walked across the kitchen in her nightshirt. She was upset. He wondered why he was so sure of that. She was too far away for him to make out the look on her face. She took a knife out of a drawer, cut something up and put it into plastic containers. Her movements were fast in their execution but as if chopped into sections; she dropped the knife — he heard the blade hit the floor — she took two potholders from a shelf on the wall, wrapped them round the handle of the kettle steaming unsteadily over one of the gas rings and poured water into two cups next to the stove. The taller of the two girls entered the room. Her mother turned round and threw something she must have had in her hand all along onto the table, a necklace, and the girl flinched and grabbed at it. It looked as if she was picking up thin air, and she said nothing.

Not much later a scuffing sound along the asphalt, a dragging of heels. The butcher's daughter, a fat, almost grown-up child, walking to the driveway. The school was only a few hundred yards away but the girl left home twenty minutes early every morning. He couldn't understand how anyone could be so fat. Her thin, short hair and her astoundingly slim hands seemed not to belong to her at all, and her tiny eyes dreamt of another, long-expired self trapped inaccessibly inside the fat.

Suddenly a loud crash, as if a heavy glass object had fallen to the ground and smashed.

You haven't got the faintest idea what your daughters get up to! yelled the landlord's wife. If you ever knew!

Stop it!

She sits by the window with that young Dörr in the afternoon, when they meet up, don't you ever see that?

They're kids. They're just playing.

And the bed!

What bed?

His bed. It's by the window.

Stop it! You're getting hysterical!

The landlord's voice was usually calm and very low but there was something else in that last sentence, a sharp tone, military, although he spoke quietly.

The old man knew that way of speaking. He only heard it rarely now and he found it unpleasant, a relapse to an earlier way of speaking.

And back then, something jeered inside him, what was it like then, did you find it unpleasant then too? He listened inside himself for an answer but none came. All that came was silence.

He stroked his hand across the cold fabric of the bedcover, looking at the window frame next to him and the crest of the roof opposite, black in the darkness. When I close one eye, he thought, the window frame covers the ridge of the roof, and when I open that eye and close the other it sets it free again. That bothered him. It had always bothered him that two eyes never saw the same thing, even though they belonged to one person.

The first thing he'd had to do when he arrived in the house that spring was to replace the kitchen window. To be precise, there hadn't been a proper window there at all, just a frame holding remains of glass and covered with cardboard, fastened to the wall with a loop of string wound round a nail. The previous inhabitant must have lived that way for years, perhaps decades; it was as if the kitchen had been blacked out.

It was the only window at the front of the building. He couldn't stand the fact that the modern double-glazing barely let in any sounds, that he could no longer hear footsteps from the road, the cars or the trams, so he had gone to the kitchen window first thing that morning to open it, as he usually did. He took a saucepan, filled it with water and immersed the water heater in it, as usual. He waited for the water to heat up, saw it getting cloudy and heard something but then he realized it wasn't the sound of the water but footsteps on the gravel.

The house was set back several yards from the street with two horse chestnut trees growing on either side of the garden, separated by a narrow path. On a calm day they blocked his view almost entirely but on that morning blasts of air blew the leaves about, leaving gaps.

The pub was closed at that time of the morning. Next to the entrance was a wooden model of a chef, with a blackboard obscuring his belly. The night's rain had blurred the writing from the previous day, Steak au . . . was all it said, everything else was just blurred streaks, between which he thought he made out fractions of letters and number fragments, chalk signs in a colour that looked like mist.

The landlord's older daughter was standing in the doorway. He first noticed the top of her head and her hand removing a hair clip from the back of her neck. Her arm was thin and tanned. She shook her head. Her hair leapt onto her shoulders. She took a hesitant step, seemingly waiting for something that she didn't want to turn round for.

He watched the Dörrs' son jump over the wall into the front garden before the girl saw him. She jumped in shock to find him squatting in front of her, blocking her way to the garden gate.

He was wearing his volunteer fireman's uniform, blue trousers and a blue jacket with brass buttons and epaulettes stuck onto his slim shoulders like slings.

Wait, he called out. Where are you going?

She looked past him, first to one side and then to the other, and hopped from one foot to the other as if trying to dodge an obstacle.

To school, where else?

He could only see her back and the nervous gesture with which she pushed the school bag hanging over her shoulder on one side far back, almost onto her back.

What time do you get out of school today?

Same as usual.

The lad was very restless now.

I'm going to be a fireman, he said.

How nice for you, she replied. I hear it pays well.

Sure, you bet it does. But not here—I want to be a professional fireman, and they only have them in really big cities, like New York.

You'll need to learn better English for New York.

The lad took a few steps backward to the tree trunk, not taking his eyes off the girl, and picked something up from behind it.

For you.

A small bouquet of pansies, purple and yellow, wrapped in silver foil.

I don't want them.

He turned away. His face looked red, a suspicious glint in his eyes, not looking at the girl any more now. She opened the gate while he stood there, his head hanging. His hand still held the flowers. He lifted them up and stared at them without a trace of reflection. Then a horse chestnut fell on his head. He didn't flinch, picking it up, enclosing it in his fist, pressing down on it and gazing firmly at the garden gate, behind which the girl turned the corner a few steps on and disappeared into a side street.

The old man thought back. Was it important to remember the two of them? Did they have something to do with the stranger?

I've lost the thread, he thought. He could tell he wasn't feeling well. His eyesight was like looking through grey now, sometimes it seemed to be a flickering and then a kind of hachure was suspended in mid-air like fabric, filling the space between him and the nightly contours of the room and making everything that had always been so nearby—the furniture, the walls, the way to the hall—seem unreachable.

The men from the building site were already in the trenches when he looked down at the street for the second time that day. Three builders; he could see them sweating from up at his window. Next to them grew a pile of sand, eyed by a fourth worker when he came by now and then. A white van came round the corner, stopping directly in front of them. Two people got out, helmets on their heads and ring binders under their arms, and discussed something; from time to time they consulted their notes and then they pointed back at the trenches, their arms making expansive movements to indicate lines.

The tram came, turning off Rödelheimer Landstrasse into the tight curve of Alt-Rödelheim, halting at the stop outside number seventeen, and then it lurched into motion again to lumber slowly past towards Lorscher Strasse but it was stopped by the white van blocking the tracks. The driver rang his bell. One of the men in helmets raised a hand, got behind the wheel and moved the van forwards, then he braked and turned round to the tram driver and called out something. It seemed that another car was blocking the way, nearer to the crossroads.

There had been a strange shop opposite the house for a few weeks now. There was no sign outside, no window decorations and it didn't seem to have fixed opening hours. He could see inside unhindered, into a large, white-painted room containing nothing but a few chairs, crates, an old chest of drawers exuding strings of hemp and scraps of coloured crepe paper and two old car tyres fastened to the ceiling with ropes. A woman and a man with very long hair went in and out every day, and he often saw children.

What was it about that place? he thought. He couldn't remember; perhaps it was something important.

And there was another image: the tram, the bent frame of the current collector stiff with dirt, the house opposite with all its windows and shutters opened at that time of day, featherbeds hanging out of the windows to air, the advertising pillar protruding above the roof of the tram. Pigeons gathered on it in the mornings; he could see them in his mind's eye—their tattered grey bodies, their restlessness.

In the house next to the shop lived a handicapped child, a boy. Like him, he often sat at the window; in the early hours of the morning he would push himself outside with a pale-blue quilt, which he folded on the windowsill slowly, with great concentration. He sometimes wondered whether the boy was sent to air the quilt at that time of day or whether he took the quilt to the window as an excuse to spend ages staring at the street, as he seemed never to leave the house.

The boy had waved excitedly that morning, and then he'd called something out that sounded like . . . eece! . . . eece!

Something startled him now and he felt for something, not knowing what. His fingers suddenly seemed cramped and difficult to move. What was it? What had the boy wanted to say?

Ten o'clock. The postman came up the stairs and put the newspaper through the letterbox. The old man had placed a chair in front of the opening so that the post wouldn't fall on the floor. He got up from the breakfast table to fetch the newspaper and went into the hall, where he saw that the chair was missing. Bending down was more difficult than walking. He had to lean his crutches against the wall first and then inch his legs apart until his hands touched the floor, and that took a while.

By the time he was back in the kitchen the coffee was no longer hot. Annoyed, he laid the newspaper on the table, cast a hasty glance at it as it lay leaning against the toaster open to the last page, miscellaneous; he remembered a large-scale photo, seals clubbed to death on a pallet in bloodstained snow, and a second, slightly smaller picture, a shot of the Voyager space probe.

Why hadn't the chair been there? The helper from the welfare centre, Mrs Mest, had moved the bed the day before and then got out his winter bedcover, and he'd watched her, sitting on that chair, which she'd fetched for him of course.

Now he felt large beads of sweat on his forehead and wiped them away but new ones followed instantly.

She had pulled his thick duvet out of a large plastic bag and shaken it; he remembered his horrified gaze at the incontinence stains on it, hideous dried-up lakes that formed unappetizing craters at the edges where the liquid had gathered. But she seemed not to have noticed his look, or perhaps she simply wanted to overlook it, just like the stains themselves.

She was a small, delicate woman with thin, slate-grey hair. She wore it in a small bun at the back of her neck, covered over by a net, and above that a starched white cap.

He watched her, that day, making up the bed in silence. She was almost his age; they could have chatted about something or the other but they never did. He would have understood it with a much younger woman, he would have accepted it, but with her he found it hurtful.

The older he got, the more difficult it seemed to be to meet people of his generation. When they came across one another and made contact, they were calls from a great distance. Fifty years ago he'd have laughed and joked with her, he'd have tried to touch her shoulders, which he liked a great deal—slim, very straight, very forceful shoulders—but yesterday he had simply followed her movements mutely, sitting stiffly on the chair.

At about eleven there were loud noises in the yard. He heard several men's voices, short sentences, laughing, then more words and laughter again.

You can get the hinges from Heuss, someone said.

On Radilostrasse?

Don't know what the road's called. The house just before the level crossing, I mean.

Two hinges?

There were three of them: the butcher, the landlord and a man with his back to him. He was speaking now, holding up two fingers. The old man was sure he didn't know him; he was short, five foot five at most, and looked Mediterranean.

Come on, Pinto, what do you think? Of course two hinges.

The slim man shrugged and laughed, a hard, cheerless laugh.

Or what do they do in your country?

Don't know.

What d'you mean don't know! The butcher's huge palm, visible from the side, landed on the man's shoulder.

You do have doors in Portugal, don't you? Cellar doors?

Sure.

The butcher's hand slipped down slightly and then slapped the man called Pinto on the upper arm.

Sure. We have them in the garden but only one door, into the house.

You mean a shed.

Yes, cellar.

No, that's a shed. A cellar is down below. How many hinges?

Huh?

On the shed door?

Two.

There you go then. Get hinges, big ones!

Later the landlord and the butcher walked past the building to a fence in the area of the plot that he couldn't see from his vantage point. They came back with a stack of planks. Long planks, carrying them between them with the landlord at the front. They walked to and fro several times; he remembered scraps of conversation between their shuffling feet and the slamming of the wood on the asphalt.

One thing you ought to know . . . I can't say, it's all your risk.

Yes, I know the regulations.

. . . of course, I know . . . why then?

We have to help ourselves.

That's what I always say, no one else is going to, that's always the way.

True, no need to hold your breath. One metre ten.

You think he'll fit in there? One metre twenty, yeah.

Or one ten.

The men leant over a sketch. The landlord took out his folding measuring stick. The wood was marked in black.

They worked at a leisurely pace. Around noon sunlight crept across the roof of the butcher's bungalow, the tarred felt blurring before his eyes when he stared at it too long. The old man remembered the many stones mixed into the tar, small, glinting spikes that refracted the hot light.

He heard them sawing, banging, hammering. It was so hot that the butcher took his shirt off.

They cropped the planks to a man's length. Once they had finished the first five, the man they called Pinto came back, placing the hinges and two metal fittings for a padlock on the table.

Let's have a look and see if we've got the length right, said the landlord with enthusiasm. He held one of the planks up and positioned it next to the short, slim man, who gave a polite smile.

Pinto comes up to my chest. Should be fine.

What do you say about these commie criminals, Pinto?

Terrible.

What would you do with 'em?

Lock them up.

Jail? That's no use. That's no use in this country. They can do whatever they like there.

Right. Our jails aren't proper prisons at all.

More like convalescence homes.

TV and hot food every day, and then they smuggle weapons in and all. Call that a prison?

Not me.

Me neither.

Better to just chop their heads off. Yes, sir.

Off with their heads.

They placed six planks alongside each other and then nailed three more across them in a Z-shape. The landlord fetched the padlock and hung it on the loop of the mounting to see if it fit.

That's great. Not even a bull could get that open!

He took three beer bottles from under the table.

They clinked bottles.

How was your time in the army?

I didn't have to do national service. Too overweight.

If you say so, replied the landlord. It's up to every man to choose.

Back then in Russia we were billeted in a town hall once. Straw on the ground, salt sacks as pillows but at least we had a roof over our heads. And there was one lad who did terrible farts. Eating, resting, washing, all so crowded together, you can't even imagine it nowadays. We didn't get much sleep, us soldiers. And we were all scared shitless, and then someone goes and takes your last bit of peace.

Pinto turned away. The butcher didn't reply.

They stared at the labels of the beer bottles.

So one night we grabbed the lad. He was only young, like me back then, I don't know what his name was, forgotten. And before he could even wake up properly we were holding onto him and pulling his pants down, and the lad thought he was having a bad dream and he started hitting out at us but still asleep. We could sleep anywhere back then. We were always tired. You soon got used to that, sleeping in trenches, sleeping at the edge of the road, sleeping standing up. I knew some, they even fell asleep at mealtimes.

The butcher still made no comment. He drank, then removed the bottle from his lips, frowning as he inspected the round opening from which foam dripped slowly onto his fingers.

So we grab him, pull down his pants and hold a lighter to his ass. It was a huge laugh but the lad wouldn't calm down afterwards. The only way we could stop him from telling on us was on condition that all of us had to have a go as well, so what could we do? We all lie down like him, every last one of us, in a nice long line. Lighters to our backsides, and measure the flame. I've still got the scar to this day.

So what about farts? asked the butcher. Do they burn then?

The landlord grinned. That depends.

On what?

Depends what you've been eating.

The night seemed endless. The old man felt wide awake. He tried to understand what darkness was, how merciless and absolute it was—nothing could chase it away. You could only ever light up tiny parts of a darkness like that, every light source ridiculous in comparison to the sun. Lamps, even very strong ones, had a light that was limited, its end foreseeable with the naked eye.

He was thirsty now. Another tram passed outside; he heard it rumbling round the corner at the place where the road took a curve outside the house, a single carriage heading for the depot. There was a gap of a hand's width between the bedside table and his bed, into which he slipped his shoulder. He stretched out his arm, pushed it along the wall behind the bedside table and grasped hold of the side edge of the washbasin. The loud ringing with which the tram always announced its arrival before it turned the corner during the daytime was missing, and the screech of the brakes was weak too. He stretched a little further, extending his arm as far as he could, and felt his jaw crack with the effort. The tram turned the corner outside the house unspeakably slowly. The carriage must be empty; he thought he could tell by the type of tremors it went through as it turned, a hollow, tinny rattle.

He clenched his teeth more firmly and felt the spindle top of the tap on one of his fingers but he couldn't budge it. There was an empty water glass by the side of the basin, still stained from the previous morning. He breathed out, got a hold on the tap, swayed it in his direction, turned the tap and listened for a while to the water flowing down the plughole and the tram moving off.

And then he suddenly thought, I can't have seen the stranger in the morning, hotel guests don't arrive until the afternoon and then leave the next day. Rödelheim is only a suburb between motorway bridges and allotment gardens, no one stays here voluntarily.

He coughed.

He thought.

What about him, was he here voluntarily?

He thought about what voluntariness was. He came to no conclusion. Was it a series of circumstances? Something that gave you the possibility to apply your own will, your own judgement, without the compulsion coming about to take a false action or, even worse, a pointless action? Or was it the opposite, the inner freedom to take your own decision at any moment, even in situations in which you seemed to have no choice at all?

The former owner had left the house to him at her husband's request. His name had been Müller, forename Karl; he had gone missing in action on the eastern front in '43.

Now he drank, at last. The water trickled between his fingers, ran along his neck, seeped into his shirt.

It made no sense that he was the beneficiary. He had no successors and he'd soon be dead himself.

And Müller of all names; there were thousands of them. He had only the faintest idea of who the man was but he was not sure even of that.

Receiving the will had torn a hole in his life. Sometimes it seemed like an opening that he could see into but only ever for a brief moment. Only to guess at the unfathomable depths that it held for him.

The weeks that followed had been a phase of incredible retardation. He had spent hours sitting in his flat, on the edge of a kitchen chair, incapable of moving a muscle. He'd understood for the first time what the expression stiff with fear really meant, that stiffness was the nature of fear, a feeling of inner acceleration, to be precise, while all else round him passed slowly, unbearably slowly.

He had gone to a Wehrmacht archive. He had laboriously paced long rows of hanging registers, papers documenting places, deployments and men's actual or presumed causes of death, all bearing the name it said on the will, but that had brought him no confirmation. Only further speculations and unanswerable questions.

He had looked at pictorial lists of men missing in action, thinking that a photo might jog his memory but that had not been the case; he had not recognized anyone.

If you looked at too many of these pictures the impressions began to overlap. At some point he only noticed the details by which one picture resembled others that he had looked at before.

He screwed his eyes up and tried to keep them that way for a while: not properly closed and not open.

He remembered the village he didn't know the name of. He wanted to keep thinking of the previous day, forced himself to think of the previous day, but he couldn't. He saw himself walking along a path, with a switch of cable in his hand. Behind him, a truck was on fire. The cable beat against his knee, cold wind blowing the smoke at his rear.

What's that supposed to mean, you don't know what the village was called, said a voice. You can't fool me. You always remember things like that.

He jerked in astonishment. As his sleep had grown lighter over the years he had heard all sorts of things in his flat in Berlin: the creaking of the floorboards, the old metal windowsills, the humming of the electricity meter and the distant shouts of every drunk outside. But it was different here. Here he sometimes heard things that his rational mind knew could not exist. Strange murmurings and other sounds from the deep crack across the wall in the hallway. An ugly, arch-shaped gap—when he took possession of the property the lawyer had told him it ran all the way down from the top floor and came from previous inhabitants' attempt to dig an air-raid cellar under the actual basement after the last severe raid on Frankfurt, disregarding the building's construction. And sometimes he heard the woman who had lived here before him for thirty-five years. When he thought of the worn-down thresholds or the stain on the living-room floor where her sofa had once stood, he saw her sitting there and heard her footsteps as she walked from the living room into the kitchen and into the bedroom and the bathroom and back again, always alone.

Now he looked round. His eyes alighted on a large trunk, mute and black and blocking a third of the small room where he slept, but the voice was not coming from there. And he turned his head slightly and looked at the mess between the trunk and the small wooden bench he put everything on, a little sun lamp, a pile of recipe magazines, a shoebox he kept old medicines in. Why had he brought these things here with him when he moved? He stared at them; they exuded dust and indifference. And then he looked over at the door, thinking about how he had pushed it open a few hours ago, only half open, to crawl into the room. He desperately wished for a gust of wind that might move it. The window was open but no wind came. And he was overcome by fear that·he would never see the door any other way than this, half-open.

His gaze moved onwards to the small chest of drawers to the left of the door, on top of it brushes and a folder where he kept old documents. The voice had not come from there either. From the washbasin, his eyes wandered down to the outflow pipe beneath it, getting caught on the pipe for some reason he didn't understand. He listened—yes, he had heard something, he was quite sure now, a hollow, splashing sound. The tap was dripping. It was a perfectly normal, old metal tap, covered in soap stains. He focused on the tap's opening, waiting for the next drip; it took an eternity to come. And then when it dropped down it sounded quite different this time, a loud, booming sound, in a metallic space that got larger and larger, was much larger now than the pipe, a cave in which the drip weltered heavily and noisily downwards like a huge mass, until the echo disappeared into the depths somewhere at the bottom, at the end of that pipe, that endlessly long pipe.

I left school at fourteen, he called out, they didn't teach us any foreign languages. I could never remember those foreign place names.

He was not quite sure whether sounds even came out of his mouth. If so, they crumbled away in the silence of the room.

And anyway, the main thing—he continued—was the atrocity of perhaps dying at any moment, having to live with that!

He cast a glance towards the grey door; it still hadn't moved. He suddenly had the feeling something was not right about those words.

He stared into nothingness.

He saw eight houses, all of them empty, and a barn. No, it wasn't a barn, it just looked like one at first glance; it was a long, low, wooden building with a flat roof and very small windows. He saw himself opening a bolt, taking a step back with his gun in his hand. Eight times; the ninth time, the door was only pushed to. He saw tree trunks with planks nailed across them, in front of them a path, a pile of sand. He saw the mark left by part of the door in the sand, clear and not blown away.

In the corridor was a large chest, on the chest a petroleum lamp. Next to the lamp was a pile of something, something soft, cold and damp, wrapped in cloth. He laid his hand on it for a moment as he passed.

Then he heard something. It was a strange sound, an insistently unremarkable, rusty noise in the silence. He looked around. Saw small desks, a bundle of willow rods leant carefully against the wall, a stove made out of a metal drum, huge. Above the large blackboard at the front of the room, half the paint peeled off it, was a white square framed with dust. Below it lay a bullet-ridden Stalin portrait.

He was freezing cold. But he was always freezing cold, the cold had never gone away despite the heaters after the War, the coke glowing white and, later, central heating. Despite the many summers he'd had, something had remained. An ice-cold core, concealed unassailably inside him.

He thought for a moment. Turned his head to the stove, tracking the sound. The stove door swung on its hinge. He saw a knee, an arm. He realized he must have a dictionary. He felt for where his chest pocket had once been, almost terrified by the touch of his own hand.

Come out!

He shouted. Deeply frightened by the now-so-brittle, old-man-like note in his voice.

A hand appeared in the stove opening and someone coughed, an agonized sound. For a brief moment he saw sunlight seeping into the room, through it the outlines of a rifle barrel as if from nowhere, a shadow on the wall. In the next second it had vanished again, just as spectrally.

A man crawled out of the stove.

It was someone of his age, strangely close as he stood there before him, with thin, blond receding hair. His padded jacket was smeared all over with soot.

The old man felt something running along his legs, warm at first, wetting the fabric of his pyjamas. *Our fault*, it hammered in his head. *Our guilt, our fault.*

He looked past the man, through a window. It had begun to snow. Tiny, whirling flakes that were still faltering undecidedly above the roofs of the abandoned houses. There was a shed behind the house. The door hung open, tools on the wall, empty grain sacks piled neatly in front of them. The trenches next to it: short, very short, exact, square. As if cut out with scissors. There was a spade in the last hole, which was not yet deep enough. He was absent now, so absent. Why am I still here? he thought, or perhaps he called it out. It sounded like an echo, like something he had already heard. Why am I still here? He opened his eyes wide, incredulous, feeling things once driven back now creeping up on him again.

There had been something there, in that corridor, he knew it, he had walked past it. He didn't want to see it again. He didn't even want to think of it.

The light in the yard went on.

He started, raised his head and listened. But he heard nothing, no footsteps. Only the sound of the water from the tap, running endlessly into the sink.

At one o'clock, he thought now, the man from Meals on Wheels had come with his lunch, as usual. He had treated him to a schnapps.

At half past two he'd gone downstairs; that was as usual too. His crutches had been leaning on the window to the butcher's processing room. Behind a barred pane of glass he could see into a short hall, and behind it came the windowless, brown-tiled room where the butcher worked on the meat. The blood had evaporated by that time, the machines were at rest. He saw the freestanding polished table with the empty drainage groove in his mind's eye now, in the middle of the room on rollers like a mortuary slab or a stretcher, saw the hose hanging with water creeping out of it in greasy, branching lines towards the plughole, the large meat vat and long black salamis hanging on hooks, crowded together like time made durable. As he went to turn away he spotted something moving in the shade of the shiny chrome vacuum-packing machine. It was the butcher's daughter, leaning over the mirror-like metal of the machine's casing, turning her head, combing her hair. She applied lipstick to her cheeks and then smudged it with spit to a grotesque, very bright red, and then she extracted something white and crumpled from her pocket and held it aloft. His eyes widened incredulously: a condom. She gazed at it like a rare find. Deliberately, she turned on the tap, washed it, turned to the machine, placed it in the middle and pulled the lever.

He held his breath. No, he was wrong, there were footsteps after all. They didn't seem to come from any particular direction. A car door slammed, another opened with a quiet squeak. The rain had set in again and filled the air. It fell on all the surfaces in the night-time yard, sounding different on each one. It drummed on the car roofs, slapped onto the bicycles and tin drums and bins, moistened the weather-beaten rush matting on the balcony of a vacant flat. It was probably spraying underneath the roofing opposite, gathering in puddles on the old table the men had used as a workbench and then put under the canopy. He imagined the rain dissolving the fine, almost white shavings they had left behind as they worked, thin shreds of wood that had stuck fast in a couple of corners and the drains and couldn't be swept away.

In his last year in Berlin he had met a man: Heinz. They used to sit on a park bench together sometimes. Heinz had told him that rain was a catastrophe for the blind; they couldn't make anything out when it rained. That made sense to him. It was impossible to place the footsteps he heard any more precisely but there were footsteps. Crazy how the rain blocked his hearing— Heinz was right. A blurred shuffling, breaking off abruptly and then setting in again, was all he could hear, and he could hardly make out where exactly it came from in this tapestry of water sounds, but it was definitely footsteps.

Why did they unsettle him so? He was used to noises like that; there was a lot of traffic through the yard, children played there, there was always something going on at the rear exits from the shops during the day. It took a while for him to realize what it was. They were the footsteps of someone who didn't want to be heard.

He grabbed the handle on the window and pulled himself up by it. It was almost a reflex; he executed the movement without thinking, feeling no pain at all.

He felt himself trembling.

Something appeared before his mind's eye — a spectrally clear cutting from a picture, a very small section. He'd have to take a step back, mentally, and turn round, walk round it, to see the whole thing, but there was no time for that now. He tried to push the impression away again but failed. He saw the skeleton of a wooden observation platform, nailed together on tree-trunk stilts, intersected struts, crosspieces above wet ground. And he saw a man walking with swaying, ungainly movements because he was so thin; it looked different from a normal person walking. *I recognized him*, he thought, but he didn't know why; he wasn't supposed to know the men there. The bark had not been stripped from the wood for the watchtower — the trees had been hastily and messily felled. Torn, white fibres protruded from the ends of the trunks, and at the point where the stilts entered the forest floor the snow was dirty, criss-crossed by tyre prints from trucks. He shouted out, shook himself, ran his hands across his shoulders, head and arms, but he knew it was useless. The dust of the past was invisible. There was no hope of shaking it off.

Cautiously, he stretched his head forward. He couldn't see anything outside in the yard at first glance, only the building as usual, leaning silent and grey. A gust of wind at the entrance had loosened the rope that linked the two posts marking the beginning of the plot like posts for a toll bar. The brown noose had soaked up moisture and rolled through a succession of shallow, round puddles, driven by the wind. Faded traces of a hopscotch game blurred on the black goose pimples of the tar. He heard the squeaking, lurching sound of a window shutter and saw a shadow detaching itself awkwardly and reluctantly from the opposite entrance. Two thin bare legs appeared in the light; dirty feet in brown men's sandals. The boy from the house opposite took a step, contorted his long back towards the shutter and grabbed at the wood. Everything about him seemed too long: his arms, his legs and even his fingers, which got a poor grip and slipped off the shutter.

A picture occurred to him that he had seen outside a church a few years after the War. It had consisted of two parts, a charcoal drawing. Two men sat facing one another on chairs, in the background a table laid with steaming bowls and dishes. The two figures held glasses in their hands from which they could not drink. It was only clear why at second glance: their lower arms were too long. You could see clearly that they'd be unable to eat either. The second part of the picture showed them feeding each other. He had found it repulsive and ugly but from time to time he remembered the drawing. Were they even men in the first place? The question arose again now at the sight of the picture in his memory.

They were such crippled figures, and they had something neither male nor female about them.

Young Dörr had retreated to the shadows again. He was sitting across the entrance step, his legs propped against the doorframe, and lighting a cigarette. His torso was slouched forwards, his head drawn in, his chin pressed to his chest. The hand holding the glowing tip of the cigarette was resting on the top of his head.

The old man tried to stay calm. But he could feel tension building up beneath the enforced calm. He thought of things he'd been taught in the War that he had never forgotten, the implementation of tiny strategic plans, the ability to get an overview of bare or complex terrain, to distrust apparent calm and motionlessness. You could shield individual actions from several viewpoints by drawing mental lines from the starting point of their movements to points that were dangerous or hard to see. The lad in the entryway gave a loud belch. His body had concealed a beer bottle, only now becoming visible as he swung his legs forwards away from the wall. At almost the same moment the bottle fell over, a loud, hard thud. The old man felt his head jerking forwards, his eyes drawing together, scanning the section of the yard in two semicircles. Behind the parked car, a head had been visible for an instant, quickly withdrawing again. The boy hadn't noticed anything. He was drunk and he swayed in his movements. He had put the bottle upright again, wiping it on his shirt and licking the leftover beer off his fingers. Then he reached into his trouser pocket and fetched something out, something the old man couldn't make out. The other figure came out from behind the car and took a step into the long shadow cast on the cobbles by the car in the light from the entry to the house opposite. It was definitely the stranger. A harried-looking man walking bent forwards, steeped in darkness up to his chest, he was carrying a cardboard palette.

The old man heard the hard, echoing clack of the timer switch in the opposite stairwell. The light at the entrance was just about to switch itself off. He looked over at the oval, dim lamp above the door, on which someone had mounted the house number in black adhesive strips. A narrow, crooked sixteen. The curves of the six consisted of crinkled lengths of tape bunched up against one another. Then the light switched off. He was confused, having stared too intently at the light. For a moment everything outside lost its contours. He closed his eyes. The number flickered behind his closed eyelids, in bright white fragments, and behind it the darkness continued, a spaceless, brown-black fabric, cold energy from weakly glimmering dots.

The stranger was climbing the stairs now. He heard his soles scraping on the stone steps and he heard him passing his own front door, resting his burden on the banisters. The fire door was pushed open, giving a quiet squeak, the handle hitting the wall twice.

I should have locked up right away, thought the old man, speaking it very loudly into his cold bedroom. He saw little clouds of steam in front of his face, although he knew that couldn't be; it was only September. He put a hand to his mouth, blew out his cheeks, blew on his cold fingers until the insides, even his bones, seemed to get warm, and then he quickly removed his hands from his face to stare at his receding breath for a while. He repeated the process a few times but there was no more steam to be seen. His fingers felt colder than before now, and his breath, which had been warm and damp, dried on his skin leaving a clammy feeling.

The lad stuck his cigarette in one corner of his mouth. He was sitting with his back to the side wall of the entrance again. The cigarette lit up his lips, only weakly. He took the lighter out of his shirt pocket again, shook it, and then he shoved his thumb over the side edge to make it spark. There was a dart of flame. A silver necklace with a pendant dangled from his hand; a tiny heart, it reflected the fire's shine, a teardrop-shaped glow. The boy looked at it for a few moments, let go of the lighter and tugged at the chain. The rip was not audible but the old man could see the lad draw back his arm and hurl it away, and then a weak, very hesitant scratching at the rear of the car.

Half past two. That was the time he had picked up his crutches and set off towards the river.

The river, the Nidda, the old man was back there again now, seeing himself standing by the bridge. He looked at the place where the water flowed over an artificial incline, saw small eddies round the shapeless rocks in the riverbed, which swirled up rubbish and the occasional dead fish, saw the deposits from three decades' worth of toxic foam, smelt the noxious miasma of the dried yellow clumps clinging to the concrete banks and slants of the weir and to the bushes.

The bridge led to the park. He was almost there now, looking through the oval barred opening in a sandstone wall surrounding the park, directly onto a small building. A house with no windows, its entrance boarded up. 'Brentano's Garden House', read a sign above the entrance. Often visited by Goethe, once a meeting place for the Romantic poets.

On the front wall by one of the two entrance pillars was a white, rather stained spot. The parks and gardens authority regularly sent someone to paint over scribbles on the bases of walls and buildings. He knew, as he passed it almost every day, that there had been a swastika here first of all, scored into the plaster with some kind of charcoal; later someone else had gone over it with a large red star. Then the authorities had come along with white paint but that just made the place stand out all the more, and if you came closer, at least if you knew what had been there before, you could still see the dark of the red shining through and the ugly scratched corners of the symbol it contained.

It was at exactly three—he remembered that because just as he was about to enter, a child in the park suddenly shouted, telling his mother loudly, Come on, it's three o'clock Mummy, let's go—that he noticed something, something from the other side of the road, from the parapet of the bridge. He turned round. There was a very unusual rattle. At first he thought it came from the building site, where men were heaving wooden supports into the road but it was very nearby. And not a rattle, he remembered that now, more of a striking sound that had confused him, metal striking metal, mingled with something else that he didn't understand, something compelling.

There was a man standing there with his back turned, looking down at the water. He was wearing a suit, his hair shining as if he was covered in sweat, or was it wet? He held a men's handbag in one hand, and with the other he was beating something against the parapet in a confusing rhythm, some object the old man couldn't identify.

It was hard to tear himself away from the sight. The beating went on as he carried on walking, even seeming to get louder, but that wasn't possible, he realized that; it must be an echo inside him.

On the second, smaller wooden bridge after the weir were two anglers, Greeks or Italians, sitting on folding stools, blinking at the sun and smiling at him. He felt the tranquil sight engendering a desire for peace in him, a painful feeling; he did his best to shake it off. One of the men got up, spat his cigarette butt in the river, waited a while for it to fall into the water and drift towards the weir, and cast out his line.

Some days he made it to the end of the park, to the roller-skating rink, and then he sat down on the lowest bench in the stands to watch the girls practising. He watched conscientiously and emotionlessly as they practised their leaps. He didn't particularly enjoy the sight; he only did it to have something to do in the first place.

He was too late that afternoon. The practice session was over and girls with tight ponytails and heavy shoulder bags came towards him. Two girls who crossed his path stood still for a moment, looked round and giggled when he reached them. He blushed and looked down at himself but there was nothing there.

There was a footbridge by the roller-skating rink, leading to a kind of island. It was densely overgrown and rarely visited. He often felt drawn there, to a quiet bench at the front of the island from where he could see the back of the weir and the courtyard of the small outpost of the waterworks that kept the weir running. There was almost always a light burning in one of the building's office windows, a man in blue work clothes usually sitting there at a desk in his office. The old man liked watching him, the light of the lamp, the nondescript colour of the walls, the colourless bars of the aged net curtain—it reminded him of his years at work.

When he got there he saw a jacket draped on the bench. Next to it a long, grubby foxtail with something crawling out of it. He focused his eyes on it and saw a beetle vanishing in a flash between the cracks in the wooden beams. The foxtail was as long as a lower arm, mangy and sticky. He couldn't tell what it was used for. It looked as if someone had dragged it along behind them uncaringly for a long time and something had got stuck to the fur on every journey, all the things no one wanted to see, that he had once overlooked himself and that he had begun noticing more and more in the past few months, tiny traces of sand and dirt, sticky, whitish drops the shape of petrified saliva, food remains burred into the tangled hairs, crumbs of chalk, ash, shreds of sticky tape, traces of old blood.

He was disgusted but he couldn't turn his eyes away. Undecided whether or not to sweep the abandoned objects to the ground and sit down, he stayed standing.

The figure that came up the bank on his right cast a shadow before it fully appeared before him: a young man, brutal, perhaps dangerous, a face that frightened him. He was grinning and buttoning up his flies, blatantly and unbearably slowly.

They looked at each other like men. He had the feeling it didn't bode well when a boy looked at an old man like that. He kicked pebbles aside as he climbed up, with a jerky, reluctant, sauntering gait that seemed to be aimed against everything he brushed up against, against the stench of the bank and the river, against the bushes, the dust.

He felt the young man drawing mental lines, from himself to him and to the bench with the jacket and the foxtail on it. He obviously wanted him to make a false move. Of course, someone like him would walk round with such an obscene, dirty, bushy monstrosity, just to challenge people to take it away from him.

If he moved the boy might launch himself at him; if he didn't he'd probably begin by insulting him and then do likewise. There was no getting out of these situations.

Wait for me.

That voice. He knew that voice.

Wait! Give it back. You said you'd give it back to me, you promised.

He saw the girl struggling up out of a tangle of grey willows a little further along. At first it looked as though she was kneeling but there seemed to be a hollow at that spot between the vegetation. She didn't notice him until she was almost at the top and patting herself down; she was covered in earth with remnants of leaves from the past winter adhering to her; she looked very pale and even fatter than usual.

She blushed when she recognized him.

Hello.

The boy turned to her half-heartedly and then dropped something, bored it into the soft ground with the tip of his trainer and buried it.

He dragged himself further along the path, his heart hammering. There was no one else to be seen. Once he had left the island via the little wooden bridge a woman came towards him with two poodles. She was wearing a jacket made of grey rabbit-fur, the dogs dodging and pulling at their leashes.

Ahead of him was the gravel path leading back to the gate. It seemed endless. He turned off to the left. He was too hot. The heat created a closeness to the things round him that troubled him. He felt everything overly clearly: his swollen hands, the glassy warmth emanating from a black park bench, the entire motionlessness draped over the area.

He stopped at a pillar in the middle of the intersecting path. He faintly smelt the decaying content of a full wastebasket. *The victims of the two World Wars and the reign of violence admonish us to peace*, was written on the plinth. He leant against the upper line of letters, pulled a handkerchief out of his pocket and wiped his face. The pillar was illustrated with a girl, a slim figure in a long skirt with a dish in her hand, so roughly and artlessly carved out of the stone that he couldn't bear to look at her for long.

There was the woman from a moment before, tying her dogs' leads to a post, walking towards a clump of trees and bushes in the middle of the path, looking round to all sides, pushing a few branches aside and disappearing into the bushes; the dogs barked.

He reached the bridge again at half past three, the man still standing there. He seemed to be waiting for something, intently watching the remains of an old car tyre scraping past large stones in the water.

He was very close to him at that moment but the waiting man only half looked in his direction; he couldn't see his face clearly. Or had he looked at it after all but only heedlessly without committing it to memory?

Between the balustrade and the riverbank, only a few steps away was a kiosk, in front of it a small space divided off from the street by empty concrete plant pots. Two drunks, War veterans, sat there in the sun on upturned mayonnaise tubs. A small boy came across the bridge; it was still very warm and he was barefoot, wearing only a vest and swimming trunks. Glasses with very thick lenses divided his face into two halves; in the middle, barely recognizable, were his eyes, two helplessly blinking dots. The tar of the pavement was full of pebbles. The child clenched his teeth and hopped as he walked. He dragged an upended net bag behind him, the handles rattling against the railings.

A woman approached from the other side, coming from the station. She was young and blonde and wore large, curved sunglasses that covered much of her face.

One of the drunks, a man with no legs, saw the boy coming. He emptied his bottle and went to put it down with the others lined up beside him but then he thought better of it and waved it at the boy.

Come here! You can earn yourself some pocket money.

The boy had reached the kiosk now. He cast a glance at the drunk without replying, put his shopping net down on the counter, took his wallet in both hands and waited.

The door to the kiosk was open. The woman who owned it was sitting outside on a folding chair eating a sandwich and didn't notice the boy.

She got up, reached behind her for a cup hanging on a nail on the inside of the door, shuffled the two or three steps to a cut-off metal barrel that served as a water butt between knotted sacks at the edge of the riverbank. She took a brief sniff at the water in the barrel.

The drunk jangled the coins impatiently in his hollow fist. The woman drank. The boy's head had now disappeared entirely into the counter opening, the back of his neck touching the pushed-up shutter hanging above him like a guillotine.

He called something timidly into the inside of the hut.

The drunk was a skinny man with a dark-red face with a matte shine like snakeskin. He drew himself upright.

Come over here, I told you.

Why? said the other drunk. Leave him be.

The boy paid no heed. He had discovered the woman and waved his wallet at her. She noticed the boy, wiped her mouth, leant her head right back and looked up. In the pale-blue sky a zeppelin hung above a line of poplars behind the bend in the river. It floated soundlessly and grey, looking huge and very near by.

As the boy took a deep breath to recite his order, the War veteran threw the bottle. The brown glass twisted in mid-flight and crashed onto the base of a sunshade, the neck breaking off, the rump bursting and splinters spraying upwards, glittering like drops of water. The boy turned aside, felt for his glasses, took them off and put them on the counter. His right eye slowly filled with blood.

Meanwhile, the young woman walked onto the bridge. The man seemed to sense her approaching, a movement at the very edge of his vision, a walking, fluttering of fabric or the thin trace of smoke that moved along the railing. Something seemed to unsettle him.

The woman stopped by the railing at some distance from him and smoked hastily, and now everyone was talking at the same time and making wild gestures. An instant later she had extinguished her cigarette with her heel, turning to go, when the man made a leap and caught her, laying one hand on the back of her neck and pulling her towards him. She turned round to him with so little resistance that he almost lost his balance, and then she pulled herself away with a horrified look, screwed up a paper bag she seemed to be holding with no particular intent, dropped it over the railing and left without a word.

She walked towards the park, almost bumping into the old man. He saw her from very close up for a moment, her red-rimmed eyes, her anger, tiredness, her cheeks hot, the thin skin beneath her eyes grey, as if stretched over a layer of lead.

On his way back to Alt-Rödelheim he turned round again and watched the man stopping helplessly with one foot on the riverbank at a point that led steeply downwards, not actually safe to tread, staring after the bag as if it might contain something important and looking round nervously several times. Everyone else was still concentrating entirely on the boy, the woman from the kiosk shouting reprimands, handing tissues and a bowl of ice cubes through the serving hatch, another man who had only just come closer, and the drunks both staring dully and aghast.

Something about the paper bag had agitated the man; he stared at it just before it sank beneath the water, a ripped milk container floating up and landing on top of it, and then they were both tugged along and sank.

The old man clutched at the bedpost. A gust of cold, wet air blew in but he could feel that he was hot.

He looked down at himself, lying on his back now with his legs apart, his feet touching the end of the bed. An end made of particleboard with a metal frame. It looks like a hospital bed, he thought, there in the middle is where they always fasten the medical charts with the patients' temperature curves.

He ran his toe over the spot. What a horrible feeling, it seemed all of a sudden, to be lying down and brushing up against a board like that with your feet. Lights criss-crossed the ceiling, headlights of people returning home by night. They drove slowly down the narrow side street. He watched their progress, the drama as they flared up at the edge of the ceiling's wooden square above his head, the way they seemed to gather on one side and then slowly detach themselves from the line where the wall and the ceiling met, hesitantly, and formed a curved gleam that extended ever further along an arch towards the middle of the ceiling.

Yet another one of those strange sounds: something hard and heavy had fallen from some height, perhaps off a table. He was sure it hadn't been a dream and it was not something you could just imagine either.

He tore his mouth open. There was suddenly a kind of dizziness in his head, as if something were falling. And a moment later the dizziness turned into a hammering inside his skull, a thudding feeling to the rhythm of his pulse, and when he pressed both his fists into the hollows of his eyes the pulsing was repeated as a staccato flashing of white spots.

I have to do something, he thought. There must be something.

Where did he keep the floor plans of the house? In the cupboard under the sink in the bathroom, or was it in the hallway? No, he interrupted his thoughts, not in the hall. Perhaps in the two old cardboard boxes on top of the dusty shelf over the kitchen cupboards? He'd have to climb on the table to get to them. How was he to manage that? Impossible! He blinked his eyes. He felt, to his amazement, something like greed. He saw the plans in his mind's eye, covered in lines and faded shading on both sides and marked with incomprehensible abbreviations, he knew that still. They'd looked so complicated at first glance; the house hadn't seemed half as complex as these convoluted floor plans. Two sheets of paper, one page per floor, and they weren't in cardboard boxes, he remembered again now, they were in a round poster tube in a cupboard in the bathroom. He tried to concentrate. On the other side of the wall, a piece of furniture was shifted, probably a table, and then he heard rustling and the breaking of wood or card. In his mind he went through the fire door and along the corridor, trying to remember which of the doors it had been that the stranger had opened, and from there he thought back again, from his hallway round the corner to the room he was in now, but even after several attempts he didn't manage to conjure up a coherent ground plan in his mind. He wasn't sure whether the room the stranger had rented really did back onto his bedroom wall.

Now a chair was pushed aside on the other side of the wall. It gave him a shock. A radio was switched on and he heard the sounds of a big band through the wall, unreal, muffled, quiet. Something creaked, followed by a movement very close by, as if the stranger were pacing along the wall. He felt exhausted and confused, his knees trembling.

I have to get up, he thought, and at least check what's going on here, even if it's the last thing I do. And it seemed as if something inside him turned, almost at the same moment as he thought it, pushing his feet downwards, to that vagueness down there that was no longer the warm bed but not yet firm ground.

A sense of confusion arose, not comparable to anything he knew, but he decided to take no heed. He sensed that it was almost a law not to do so.

Where was he now? He didn't know—it seemed some kind of in-between land, made up of closeness to death and dream.

In this land everything was possible without strength. Without strength, as he realized to his surprise, everything was even easier. How light he felt now; he sensed it was not normal. He seemed to have laid his crutches aside. Yes, the time for crutches was over.

He dressed effortlessly. He felt a strange jollity. There was a broom next to the door, something to hold on to, he thought and reached for it out of habit but in the middle of the motion he thought better of it, his arm hovering in mid-air. He looked at it for a moment and then at the handle, and tittered. He imagined the broom handle cracking quietly when he put all his weight on it, concentrating on it with all the strength he had, and a moment later he heard it: a short, dry sound.

In the bathroom, he opened a cupboard. He came upon a collection of old bottles. Some were filled with liquids, their labels long since peeled off or faded. It was damp here—there must be a wet patch further back. A pair of mildewed rubber gloves lay next to a row of clothes pegs and stained cloths, open pairs of scissors and tangled wires, rusty skeletons. The poster tubes he had been looking for were on one side, brownish grey and smelling of mould. He pulled them out, shook them, whirling up dirt that flew into his mouth accidentally, and he coughed. He opened one of them. Its contents had long since mouldered away, now a smudgy mess that he could only scratch out with difficulty.

His toolbox was behind the drainpipe. He pulled it out, opened it and knelt down laboriously in front of it. For a while he gazed in indecision at the mess, running a fingertip over nails, once arranged by size, which were now all piled in together. They were black and shiny. Their tips made a pattern that looked like that of snow crystals. Heinz had told him about Soviet drillings in the Antarctic, it occurred to him, and since then, he'd said, they knew that the coldest cold was not white but black and hard as metal; under constant grinding, a dark material formed deep down on the coldest sheets: water in an as yet undiscovered fourth state of matter. The scientists' drills had had a lens and diamond tips. The diamond had broken a few kilometres down, and when the scientists removed the drill again they saw that the space it had left closed up again with great force; at one narrow spot, suddenly released from its pressure, a tiny piece of the concentrated ice had been allowed to expand again, fleeing from its black state. For millions of years, Heinz said, there had been a layer of cold under the ice in all its tons, ice under the pressure of huge amounts of other ice, which had transformed under the great weight of pressure and friction of cold moving blocks into concentrated pitch-black coldness.

He drilled his finger deeper into the pile of nails and came upon grinding, sandy dirt. Flakes of dust grew between the thin metal rods. Grains of sand, thought the old man, are nothing but particles broken off from rocks, parts of huge, once insurmountable mountains.

Behind the basin was an old bag. He opened it and took out the drill inside it, his own one, very small, an old mechanical model with a cast-iron, wooden-handled crank. He sniffed at the wood. It had a nondescript scent, musty.

His father had given him the drill in 1917, when he was a young boy. His father had lost an arm in the War and later wore a prosthesis, living another twenty years with it. The wooden limb, called a Germania arm, had a screw thread to which you could attach various appliances: a fork, a spoon, a hook, tools. The old man thought of his parents' flat, which had usually been cold, of the soups with circles of grease floating on top that he'd had to eat as a child, his father's cigar smell, the red-brown, unhealthy skin on his face and hands and the squeaking in the silence of mealtimes when he changed the ends of his prosthesis. All that was a long time ago and seemed insignificant now, and as he realized that he felt his heart lift.

He looked across at the large wall in his bedroom. In the middle, about five feet above the floor, he noticed a dent. Strange, he thought. Like an optical illusion, it was not clear whether the wall arched inwards or outwards.

He went closer, hesitating. The drill was heavy in his hand. The modern electric drills always startled him but this one was different; it would be quiet and thorough. He felt his fear, a strange, vibrating coldness beneath the roof of his skull.

What was it, just paper? He stroked one finger across the bulge, tapped at it, felt it giving way slightly under the pressure. Yes, just paper. There had obviously been a hole in the wall here for a long time — someone must have looked through it before him.

He put the drill aside, stepped closer, blinking.

He could easily make out part of the stranger's room, the light still on. He saw the foot of the bed, his feet protruding from beneath the cover, a narrow table, a washbasin. Under the table was a holdall. It was open; the old man saw clothes spilling out of it, between it parts of a cardboard box. There was an old radio as well, the kind he used to know, he'd once had one himself; Oslo, Vienna, Prague, Budapest, the black dial with numbers and names of faraway cities glowing orange in the semidarkness.

He stared through the wall until his eyes began to hurt.

A creak. The stranger must have got up. He couldn't see him directly, just a small section of the shadow cast by his legs and the bedcover as he pushed it aside.

Now he did come into view, not yet undressed, apparently not intending to sleep at all.

He switched on the radio, looked for a station, gave up and sat down on the end of the bed. His eyes flitted searchingly across the table, littered with cigarette packets, a lighter, a wallet, a bag of sweets and several ballpoint pens, and then he seemed to have an idea, leaning forwards, pulling the holdall out between his feet and ripping off a piece of the cardboard box inside it.

The old man ran a hand across his eyes. If he looked at one spot for too long brown and black threads danced on the surface of his vision, as if they were floating on an invisible fluid.

The stranger turned to the table, picked up a pen, smoothed out the card, drew something on it, took an empty cigarette packet, closed it and bent it straight. He took the other two cigarette packets as well, putting them all in specific positions on the cardboard. And then he moved them round like toy cars according to a certain plan: one of them drove straight ahead like on a wide, fast road, one was parked to one side, the third suddenly turned off a side street and crashed into the first, and then the second one, the parked car, joined it, accelerating and blocking the road. He repeated the procedure several times over until the first of the cigarette packets was crumpled from the crash, and then he picked it up, laughing, threw it up in the air and watched it landing in another corner of the room.

The old man started with fear. A crossroads lined with suburban villas reared before his mind's eye, at night, a picture from a camera. He saw a car standing still on the road, a second one with its boot smashed in, a pram, a garden sprinkler. He wasn't sure what these things meant; he pushed them away.

The stranger seemed to have a sudden idea. He leapt up, looked round for something, reached for his jacket that was outside the old man's view, and went through the pockets for something, perhaps the keys—something jangled a moment later. Impatiently, he tied his shoelaces, tugged his shirt straight, went to the washbasin, washed his face, ran his hands through his hair and left the room. He closed the door loudly and walked down the stairs with hurried footsteps gradually moving away.

The old man held his breath.

A car turned into the yard, driving over the manhole cover in the driveway, a dull, very low sound making the walls tremble. He heard the sliding door of a van and men's voices whispering quietly. It was the butcher's van—they were back.

In a strange gait, almost floating, he saw himself
walking round the bed to the window. A gust of wind
must have slammed it shut. The old net curtain hanging
in front of it, affixed tautly to two rods, covered the glass
with a leafy, confused pattern, which stood out black
against the weak yellow light outside. He tried to open
it again but it seemed to be stuck, swollen from the moisture outside. He tugged at it, wondering where he was
finding the strength. Now the frame did move but only
a tiny bit, just enough so that the sounds were slightly
louder and cooler air came in through the gaps.

They seemed to be unloading something. He squinted
past the gaps in the curtain and saw two blurred figures,
one standing upright, the other bending over. They were
carrying something pale out of the van, presumably one
of the white plastic tubs the butcher used to transport
his goods.

He looked over to the stranger's car. It was still
parked, locked up—where was the man? There were no
more sounds to be heard inside the building, he must
have reached the end of the stairs long ago, so they
ought to bump into one another right now: the butcher,
the landlord and the stranger.

He felt his own agitation. I have to check, he
thought. I'll go to the door and open it and listen if he's
still there. Perhaps he's got lost, taken the wrong exit, the
one to the butcher's processing room, or he accidentally
ended up in the basement.

A moment later he was already outside, listening. What was that? A humming sound: the central heating. A strange, high-pitched buzzing.

And then footsteps again but no voices. Moving bodies, groaning. A tremor as if something heavy had slammed into a wall.

Hold it lower down, someone said—the butcher. My back, dammit.

Pull yourself together, it's all going fine, the landlord told him.

There was something else between their words. It had sounded like a dull blow.

Through the rods of the banisters, he saw the bald back of the butcher's head, the man bent over the trough. There was something large in it, wrapped in a brown army blanket.

There was the buzzing again and a semi-suppressed, gasping bark, the landlord's dog coming to the nearby front door, growling, and the landlord looked up and waved his arm as if in a helpless threat.

Shut up, you little bugger!

They shoved a lid on the tub.

That's that then.

Yes, that's put a lid on it!

Had he lost consciousness for a moment? The old man ran a hand across his face. The strange coolness of his hands gave him a start.

What a beauty, eh?

Oh yes.

The butcher's voice sounded hoarse when he was drunk.

Heavy though, isn't he? What do you reckon, how much does he weigh?

No idea.

Just a guess.

I can't tell you, I'd have to put him on the scales.

And how much is he worth?

The butcher raised his arm and gestured towards his shop.

Who knows? They laughed.

The old man closed his eyes. Now he saw a broad, bright cone of light darting across a patch of ground fenced in with barbed wire, on the edge of a wood and protruding halfway into the forest, the trees bare and weighed down with snow. It looked almost empty at first glance but he knew once his eyes had got used to the darkness he would make out low mounds of earth, and hollows, and sleeping men seeking shelter there.

Where am I? he thought.

There was the spectrally thin man, standing up, running, the searchlight wandering along the barrier. On the other side of the fence were trees, their trunks shining bright, birches. He knew they were the only ones the prisoners had not yet peeled the bark from and eaten. The thin man stuck his arm through the wire, gripped one of the tree trunks; the light gave a brief sway and then reached him very quickly, drawn by the movement as if by an invisible force.

Something boomed in his ears, gunshots. They were shooting from above. The trees swayed. The wood splintered. The man dangled from the fence.

Where am I?

He didn't know, but he knew he was not the one who shot, although it could have been him.

He was the one who recognized the face.

The men disappeared into the basement. The tub slid about and then seemed to be set down with a firm thud, and the two men were audibly angry; they seemed to have lost control for a moment because of the weight of the object. Then they came back out and one of them — he guessed it was the landlord — locked the door.

He felt his way further down the stairs, hearing their footsteps gradually receding; sensing two sentences that rose within him alternately, over and over, like different colours that wouldn't mix, or like lighting conditions that cancelled each other out: He's one of them. I have to save him.

He was standing at the foot of the stairs, in a narrow, tube-like room with a bare light bulb and three doors. He found it strange that he could move from the spot with such lightning speed in one moment and at the next crept along so unbearably slowly.

There was a small map of the area pinned to a board, framed by advertising for a few nearby shops, a cleaning rota for the stairs and the remaining scraps of an old form with only the letters 'kwart' still decipherable.

Next to that the mail boxes, brown and dented. His had not been opened for a long time now. He had put a makeshift name-sign on it when he moved in, sticking a piece of paper over the old sign, a cheap strip of stamped plastic tape; if you ran a finger along his name the old letters stood out in relief underneath: Müller.

When he switched on the light and turned round he saw the blood, a kidney-shaped pool, already darkening close to the door to the basement.

His heart thudded. He was indignant—how could it thud so loudly? It distracted him from thinking; he had to keep thinking now.

When had the stranger arrived—in the morning? The bonnet of his car had been warm when the old man had rested on it on his way home in the early evening but he couldn't tell whether it was because of the engine; perhaps the metal had simply heated up in the sun.

What had the boy been trying to say with his eece, eece, what was important about young Dörr having waited for the landlord's daughter that morning, in the front garden, and hadn't there been a man there as well, with a paste brush?

He felt his lips moving. He kept repeating the questions over and over without speaking, only forming them with his lips. Perhaps they were nothing but a trembling of his lips that was getting worse and worse, like all the questions he saw clearly in his mind's eye like question marks, whirling faster and faster in a circle, like poles on a merry-go-round. And their answers were like faces smiling briefly at him as they flew past, faces with nothing distinctive about them, faces impossible to remember. He so wished he could catch a glimpse of at least one of them and commit it to memory.

A green car.

And the wanted posters, of course. Was the stranger's photo on them? Was it him they had built the cubbyhole for? He had certainly seen wanted posters in the street but where?

Eece—eece, he repeated with a stammer. A green car. Police. Saliva gathered at the corners of his mouth and he felt his breath blowing it dry.

Yes, a green wing of a car, that morning, green like a police car. Hadn't there been police everywhere, hadn't they been handing out leaflets to pedestrians, shopkeepers, possibly to the butcher and the landlord too?

The green car was standing at the junction to the small side street and had blocked the road for the white van and the tram. And people had called out. And the tram had rung its bell but he'd taken no notice, he'd been hungry, had closed the kitchen window, laid the table as usual. He hadn't really been able to see what was going on from up there.

He was standing outside on the street now, suddenly as in a dream. But this wasn't a dream, it was something else. What was it? Waking, drifting away, a transition? Where would it take him?

He stepped out of the driveway; it had stopped raining. From a distance, as if through a veil, he saw the tram tracks. The butcher's shop was in a narrow side path between the weir and the road.

He walked up to it. But there was nothing left on the window, just traces of tape once stuck to the glass.

The blue night-lighting made all the objects in the shop appear larger and bulkier: the large scales, the chopping block, the glass-fronted counter, now empty at night save for a few crumpled napkins, bread rolls used for decorations and piled-up price signs.

He saw that the bread rolls were sprinkled with poppy seeds and sesame and attached together in the shape of a large wagon wheel; when he stared at it for long the wheel started turning.

Russian bread, he mumbled, is made of rye groats, but only half, the rest is mashed sugar beets, wood flour and dried leaves.

No, there was nothing on the window but there was something on the floor. He inclined his head to one side and pressed his face against the glass. Yes, that must be it, the poster he had been thinking of. He even thought he could decipher some of the writing: terrorists, urgently wanted.

Twelve pictures: eight women and four men. One man with a moustache, that wasn't him: too thin, and the nose was wrong too. One with glasses, very fat, and one man with thin strands of hair almost thinning to baldness. And the last picture? Yes, that must be him, a middle-aged man with inconspicuous features, scowling.

Strange how many people there were who had nothing distinctive for him about their faces, nothing worthy of a clear memory. Or was it because he was trying too hard now, too clearly to recall the expression of this person who had come so suddenly to the focus of his thought, so much so that the details of his features refused to form an overall impression, kept slipping away from him?

He spotted some numbers at the bottom edge of the poster and his left hand went mechanically to the chest pocket of his shirt where he usually kept a pen, but this time he didn't manage to grip anything. He started with shock. His chest felt like a stranger's. It seemed to be covered in something rough, the origin and nature of which was unclear, and his fingers slipped along it into thin air.

I'll have to learn the number off by heart then, he thought. I'll have to remember it at least until the telephone box on the corner.

He looked at the row of numbers but it suddenly seemed very long. He had to make a huge effort to decipher them fully in the bluish darkness of the room behind the glass. He thought of how he had learnt poems by heart as a child, a trick his mother had taught him. You had to read what you were learning out loud over and over, and at the same time you took a piece of paper and pushed it slowly along the lines from one side, reading over and over again as the paper gradually covered the writing. At the same time as that thought, something grey pushed its way slowly into his vision, between his eyes and the numbers, blotting out the numbers as he murmured to himself. He was relieved; so he could still do it, learn things by rote. But then he realized that the grey, which was square-shaped, was not just superimposing itself on the numbers but on everything he could see, and making it disappear, and he was deeply shocked. So this is it, he thought, the end of sight. He rubbed his eyes and the spectre vanished again to his surprise but he was still suspicious. Wasn't it still there, that grey square, very faint, barely visible, making the things he saw look paler and more transparent?

He turned away. A weasel streaked along the gate of the waterworks, slipping outside through the bars. He watched its progress. A window opened at the Red Cross station, an old wooden house across the road, a woman put her head out and pushed a dish outside. For a brief moment he saw the room she was standing in. There was a large white pair of scales, not unlike the butcher's scales, a small medicine cabinet containing bottles and tubes and dishes, and there was a drawing on the wall, a human body cut open along its blood vessels and nerve fibres.

He got to the telephone box. At first it looked as if someone was in there, a tall man in a hat. He felt anger rising inside him. People with no telephone of their own, who make calls at night—he knew that kind of thing, they never came to an end. He hadn't had a telephone for years either.

No, there was no one in there, just an old rag hanging over an electricity box behind the telephone booth, fluttering in the wind.

He sensed it would be nice to think of the past now. But he forbade himself from doing so. It was better not to pursue that kind of thought, just as it was sometimes better not to call to mind in a dream that you were only dreaming.

He opened the door to the booth and gazed at the large grey telephone and the small box for emergency calls, looking for ten-pfennig pieces in his pocket. He always had a couple of coins in there but this time all he could feel was a scrap of paper, with which he fumbled briefly and then pushed quickly back down again.

He picked up the receiver, pulled the emergency-call lever, heard a crackle that hurt his ears and then another, very distant sound that seemed strangely familiar to him. It sounded like the grinding of glass marbles on the sandy ground of an allotment where he had played some-times as a small boy. He could see it now, yes, the bare, unshaded plot of land with the summer heat trapped upon it, he could feel his hot hands holding more marbles and he saw the ground coming gradually closer.

Hello? Can you hear me?

He felt the wall of the telephone box against his back, and himself slipping slowly downwards. His feet struck several small alcohol bottles standing on the base below the telephone, next to pressed-out cigarette butts and something else that he couldn't quite identify—it was reminiscent of an old glove.

Where are you? Is there something you want to tell us?

He wheezed, the receiver still tightly gripped in his hand. Ash had scattered onto his knees; he brushed it off and held his eyes firm on the white traces left behind on his trousers.

Are you all right?

The voice at the other end of the telephone seemed very warm and professionally concerned.

They've taken him prisoner, he whispered into the receiver. You have to rescue him.

Yes, of course. Who exactly are you talking about?

The man in the photo.

Which photo?

Bottom right, on the wanted poster.

For a while he heard nothing, then came a movement, an expulsion of breath; he could tell the man on the other end of the telephone was leaning back in his seat.

So you think you've recognized one of the terrorists the police are looking for?

Yes.

A man from the wanted poster?

He heard tittering in the background and clinking of glasses, followed by a quiet engine sound like that of a mixer or a vacuum cleaner.

What's his name?

I don't know, I couldn't remember it, but I saw his photo.

I'm sure it's a mistake.

No, I know it's him. And he's in danger. Low music came from the receiver now. Radio music, he whispered.

It seemed to him as if he had once known the song well, and he sensed he wanted to hum along and he closed his lips. He felt that they were very dry.

The poster 'Dangerous Terrorists'?

Yes. The person in the bottom right-hand corner.

That's not possible.

I know very well I recognized him.

The person in the bottom right-hand corner, you say?

Yes, I'm quite sure.

That's a woman.

He felt something opening up in his stomach, cold and very unpleasant. And there was something else. Something that took him prisoner and at the same time weakened him, hollowed him out, a silvery fluid, it seemed to him, and it was poured into that opening, and it pulled him towards it, to the sheen and the clarity radiating off it.

He felt that he had to walk on, he must not stand still. Perhaps there was another, second wanted poster somewhere?

On, he thought, how did it go on? Half past four—he had almost reached his house. He had been walking on his side of the road but now he had to cross over to avoid the uneven ground and ditches of the building site. An acrid smell invaded his nostrils and he turned in its direction, spotting a small tarring machine on the road. Hot air had gathered above the kettle, pushed slowly along by a sullen man covered all over in sand-coloured dust, and everything above it lost its outlines and floated in the heat, things flowing into one another like in a dream.

That was when he had seen the man, on a level with the tarring kettle, coming out of the strange, empty shopfront with something under his arm, something rolled up, and holding something else in his hand—it was a paste brush.

The old man felt himself sweating.

And he thought: red. It was red.

But what was red? He didn't understand how it all fit together.

And now he was directly in front of the advertising pillar, like that afternoon, almost touching it. Strange—it was only a few yards away from the streetlamp; he ought to be able to read the posters but he found it difficult.

He ran his hand round the pillar, feeling the thick layer of all the sheets of paper pasted over one another for years, but he couldn't make anything out. He walked a little way round the pillar, staring at all the posters without seeing.

What a strange light! He looked at his hands; they shimmered in a cold, ugly green, all the scars and spots looking like dirt on them. What a colour of great cold and desolation. Where did the light come from that made everything look so alien? He looked over at the slim post on the street corner but it didn't seem to come from there—there was only a weak ray of yellow, with no great reach. And he looked up at the sky to see if it was dark, if there were any stars. But there was no sky, there was only a dull greyish-brown cloth suspended above the roofs.

He tried to concentrate, looked up, recognized a cigarette ad, a notice about a concert on the radio, an election poster for the German Communist Party, the announcement of the big white-water canoe race on the Nidda—yes, he knew that, it had long since taken place, it had been in the summer—and a large sheet of paper of an indefinable colour, covered in prints of small hands, children's hands.

Perhaps he had been mistaken, perhaps it hadn't been on the advertising pillar at all. Who took notice of all the tiny details on a harmless afternoon's walk?

Now he came to the building site. He had avoided it that afternoon—there were too many trips for his feet here, too much sand and dirt, too many uneven spots he could have stumbled over.

He watched himself crossing the tram tracks and walking towards the ditch. A gust of wind had blown; he remembered the fluttering of the awnings, a clinking sound, napkins and beer mats fallen from the tables, blown over the fence onto the pavement. Two women walking along the road had held onto their skirts.

And then there had been something *white*, something large and white had come loose from somewhere and fallen into the ditch, and one of the workers, bent sweating over the pattern of stones for hours as if over a difficult jigsaw puzzle, had stood up reluctantly in the afternoon heat and climbed into the ditch to fetch it out again.

How he ran and ran now.

So many steps for such a short distance. He didn't quite understand it but he had to keep going, it wouldn't stop.

He was slowly approaching the spot. A sign with a large post horn: cable-repair work, next to it a board laid over the hole. For a brief moment he saw only the board and men sitting on the edge with their trousers down but that couldn't be right; he rubbed his eyes and saw with relief that the rubbing of his eyes made the men more and more transparent, like ghosts.

The ditch was two metres wide and took up the entire pavement. It was edged with piles of stones covered with a tarpaulin and lamps tied together with a rope, one of them still flashing. The remains of a breakfast balanced on a paving stone. A protective glove lay clenched like a fist in the sand.

He lowered his head, looked at the sides of the trench and smelt the scent of the damp earth. Roots protruded from the gaps in the boards against the sides. If he looked at them for long he had the feeling they were growing towards him.

And there was something white too, just as he remembered it, crumpled, wrapped round an iron rod. He bent and picked it up: a piece of paper, old and yellowing.

A chart, some kind of measurements.

He read: Ration for seven days. Fats: low-fat cheese, cutlet powder. Staple food: sugar, bread, salt. German tea. The numbers were no longer legible. He grew angry, his eyes glued to the paper. *Wrong*, it hammered in his head. *We didn't give them anything. Nothing at all.*

The earth disappeared and the white came back and grew as large as a cloth, a sheet, and on the sheet were hands, his hands, but they had a strange colour to them and were very heavy. He could hardly manage to lift them.

Six o'clock. He reached the backyard. The light was evening light already, the walls and the asphalt radiating warmth. The stranger's car was in the far right of the three guest-parking spaces, in front of a flower pot.

He shuffled past it, resting on the warm bonnet for a moment. Voices came from the basement. He walked on to his staircase and could still hear them, getting louder.

Yes, someone said, this is the basement.

The sound of the words mixed with the coolness and the corky smell coming out of the barred windows at his feet. He had meant to unlock the door but he stopped still.

And the basement, you might think, is the deepest place in the house. But that's not the case here.

The voice gave a dramatic murmur. Two other voices giggled: the girls.

No, not here. Take a look at this.

At what?

The floor here, the basement floor, what colour is it?

Dark.

Yes . . . it's dark, said the voice in a silly sing-song.

And the girls giggled again.

And the walls, the doors?

Dark.

Yes.

It's all very dark. And do you think it can get any darker? He waited but no answer came.

No? Then take a look at this.

What a sound! How it made him jump, as if somewhere very far below rocks or stones were being shifted, at a depth that seemed to be not only of place but also of time.

The lad took a step aside. A hole was visible, not much larger than a manhole, black, even darker than the floor.

What is it? whispered the high voices.

The air-raid cellar.

Was he in the right place? Yes, he was standing by the entrance now.

There was the bloodstain again, dried, almost black. Wiped tracks led to the basement door.

He stepped inside.

He knew that when you entered a basement area you sometimes didn't get into the proper basement right away but to a kind of anteroom. That was where he was now, in a fairly large space divided into two, containing electricity meters and an old laundry room. He had to cross this area first to get to the way down. He had never been down to the very bottom.

He came up against a large bathtub with an old tap, his legs stroking against it, and he held onto it for a moment and looked into it, saw the wheels of an old hand-barrow that someone had thrown in there, a sack of potting soil, the plug for the old bath on a rusty chain, and smelt the limestone and the leftover soap of past times.

The electricity meters hummed on the other side of the wall. All the residents' names were written there, including his own. He stared at the names, the small cogs that measured the electricity consumption rotating, the tiny metal teeth shimmering before his eyes and threatening to blur, and below them the meters rattled away untiringly, now faster, now slower.

He stepped up to them, trembling, searching. His cog was standing still.

I mustn't stay here, he thought, and I mustn't stop thinking either.

You'll never really be gone, Heinz had said on his last afternoon in Berlin, when he had told him he'd miss the city.

You think so?

No, I know so.

They were sitting in a small stone pavilion in the Humboldthain park. They looked down at a lawn from a slight hill. Long-haired men were sitting on a picnic blanket, smoke rising between them, laughter. A Turkish boy was building a dam in a stream, piling up sticks and branches, which kept getting torn away by the water flowing sluggishly downhill. After a while his patience ran out and he began using lumps of earth. Later, as they were talking, angrier by then, he used stones.

It's down to the fourth dimension.

Heinz's theories were eccentric mixtures of science, general wisdoms and imagination; he never quite knew which of them were true.

Something to do with Einstein. But it's not all that complicated. Look.

He took something crumpled, stroked it smooth and held it up: an old shopping list he had fished out of one of his many bags — he collected all sorts of things.

Sometimes he spent the night in the park, in spring and summer. He knew the entrances to the old air-raid bunker and he knew that the local children were always trying to break in. When they emerged hours later from the world of the past, their faces proud and overheated like coal miners, lugging out army blankets, rusty surgical instruments and cans of phosphorous paint, he was lying in wait for them. He took their treasures away from them again and chased them off. He called it his work and it seemed never to come to an end. The supply of relics from the past stored in the huge, grey monstrosity on the northern edge of the park seemed never to run dry, just as there were always new children robbing it, equally pale, equally young, every year.

Just imagine the world's a piece of paper like this, Heinz said to him, and imagine you live in this paper, like in a picture. What would you be missing then?

Pretty much everything, he had replied.

No, that's not what I mean. Something more important.

More important than everything? That's impossible.

Think about it.

He ignored his comment.

You can walk along here—he ran his index finger over the paper in sweeping circles up to one end—or along here—he ran his finger downwards—or wherever you like, the paper can be as huge as you like, as big as the globe, but what would be missing?

No idea.

Think about it.

I can't think of anything.

A dimension.

A dimension?

A dimension.

Heinz had looked at him with his small, rather cold eyes, with the glow of a thirst for knowledge broken by alcohol, and then he said, We move in three dimensions in the real world.

And as he said it he pulled his thumb back and stuck it through the paper, pulled it out again and presented the hole to him.

Now what can you see?

There's something missing.

Precisely.

And what?

Call it what you like. Call it the past or call it a dead man.

I don't get it.

We here in the world of three dimensions, we move in multidimensional curves, that's perfectly normal for us.

He was getting loud now, that happened sometimes; he waved his arms round, drawing circles, stabbing through the paper several times and looking at the results, jerking the sheet upwards and holding it in front of his face with a wild gesture, with a burst of crazed laughter.

See that? The people, I mean the ones that only live in two dimensions, if they existed, I mean, they don't understand what's happened, they don't know the third dimension, there's something missing for them. This here means they've lost something! Do you get me? Lost! It's all lost!

He was yelling now. The boy in front of them sat up, shock on his face, picked up his stones and ran away.

What do you mean?

That time passes. That it passes *differently*, to be precise.

He retrieved a small bottle of schnapps from his sleeve, half empty already, unscrewed the lid and sniffed at it without drinking. For a moment it looked as if Heinz had intended to offer him the bottle, just to breathe in the scent.

An inheritance, he said suddenly, quietly.

Yes. Imagine that.

It had sounded awkward, he knew that.

You should be glad, you're not glad at all.

No, I'm not.

Do you have to move over there then? Why don't you sell the old pile?

It's not an old pile.

I didn't mean it like that.

That's all right. Maybe you can come and visit me some time.

Yes, who knows.

It's a good way away though. Eight hours on the inter-zone train.

Too far for me.

And the fourth dimension? What about that then?

His thoughts had begun drifting; he seemed not to remember it any more.

You were going to explain it to me.

Heinz groped for the bottle, which was back in his sleeve, his fingers trembling as he took the first sip.

We know that time is the fourth dimension but we can't move round inside it. And that's why everything's finite for us.

That's the only reason?

Yes, that's the only reason. We can't go backwards on the ribbon of time — the past is gone for us. People die, tear holes in our existence like in this paper but that's just the way it seems to us.

Heinz took three swigs at once. His eyes were now more bloodshot than they had been for a long time and his gaze clouded over, flitting between the lawns, the bunker, the bridges and the plastic and paper bags at his feet.

You think so?

Yes.

You mean the dead aren't really gone?

The dead aren't gone, not one of them. And the past isn't gone either.

There were the stairs, wide concrete steps with a sturdy iron railing, and it was so easy to walk down them, the old man's feet barely had to touch the ground.

He came to a corridor with various doors off it. One of them shimmered silvery, the first one on his left. He walked straight up to it.

No, it was not a door at all but a metal casing with an entrance built into a niche. And the handle was shaped like a steel club. Thin, spectral mist emanated from the padded gaps, flowing slightly above the floor and then dissolving into thin air just before a new burst of fog came out from inside, an interplay of flaring and then vanishing scraps, white but a white with no light, no brightness. The old man shifted forwards slightly. His left leg felt numb. He laid his hands against the metal. There was a strange warmth here, a stuffiness like a lack of oxygen. He heard the sound of a fan but he couldn't see it. It seemed to be hidden behind the wall; he saw the wind it produced, felt its heat, the motion of the air, saw black threads, strangely interwoven gossamers and shapeless, trembling growths driven along the corridor by the wind, floating a little way in the hot air and then getting caught somewhere or other, in dark nooks or on the colourless floor that exuded dirt. And some of them seemed to stick to him, settling on his hair and his chest. He looked down at himself but it was too dark to make anything out. He swallowed and convinced himself he could feel them there too, the growths of dirt, on his tongue, imagined it was them causing the strange scratching in his throat now, making it swell up. And imagined they were already in his stomach and causing the unsubstantial, queasy feeling he had there now.

He grabbed at his neck, hearing with a shock the gurgling sounds he was giving off. And he felt himself sweating now, sweating for the first time in hours. But he was sweating and shivering at the same time. He fumbled at his clothing, his hand wandering across the shirt he had been wearing for days, disgusted at the clammy moisture of it, and across his trousers, which felt jagged and rough and were now covered in dirt from the basement, and that disgusted him too.

He took a deep breath and swallowed, swallowed over and over.

He reached out an arm, caught hold of the handle of the cold-storage room, turned it to the left, felt resistance, shook his head and turned it to the right. It twisted with a screech. The door leapt open, clouds billowed out and he was standing in a wall of fog and cold.

It was bitterly cold after only a few seconds but that didn't bother him at all; he had the feeling that this cold was merely the equivalent of another cold that had lived inside him for decades, and that they were now linking together, the exterior cold and the interior; it seemed only consequential that it ignored the ridiculous little that was left of him.

The floating whiteness thinned out only slowly. Everything in the room was coated in a layer of iciness, which traced and enhanced the objects' contours strangely, as if ageing them. He saw a row of objects hanging from rounded hooks, and the hooks themselves were hanging from a dark metal rod attached to one wall of the room very high up, almost at the ceiling. Not objects, he corrected himself mentally, bodies. Animal bodies, of course, but still bodies or at least parts of them. Why had he thought at first of objects, he wondered. Perhaps because they were so hard and because they looked nothing like living creatures any more once they stopped moving.

He came across several tubs, *stew* was written on them and then a date, *gravy, chicken casserole*.

He had to tear himself away, that he knew; the cold was pulling him in. He was leaning against the wall, or stuck to it. He raised one arm and reached for the doorframe, from where there were still white scraps of mist escaping into the basement, leaving the room reluctantly and dissolving after a short while out in the corridor. He managed to move his body away from the wall and he took a step, pulled himself back out into the open.

He felt his way further forwards, bumping into something angular that he hadn't seen, a set of rough shelves, ancient and lopsided. Obscured, dark-brown glass jars were piled up on them and an appliance that seemed oddly familiar and yet at the same time very strange, a rubber-like formation, a mask with two giant, dirty eyes of glass, an unfinished face of porous material that led not to a neck but to a tube, and the tube curled a slight way and then hung down limply when he touched it, tugged at the object, threw it on the ground, and he laughed, a joyless laugh. It was an old gas mask.

Where was he now? A rounded, cavernous entrance, and behind it, at the end of the corridor now, he could make out something pale: wooden planks, as good as new. Yes, it was the door, the one the butcher and the landlord had put together. And he sensed he wanted to run off, right over there, and solve the puzzle, but he didn't seem to be able to, something was holding onto him, an immaterial force that guided his feet.

He was blown in there, into that entry. What a strange wind, he thought, how it has me in its grip, pushes me ahead of it, it has no physical tangibility or meaning, it seems to be the product of my consciousness alone, but still it's powerful and strong. Its effect is much stronger than anything I've been exposed to in my life.

He took a step forward, feeling the wall. It was made of soft, sandy stone; crumbs sprinkled to the ground when he scratched a finger across it.

He sat down on the floor, panting for breath. Something beneath him was set in motion, there was a rattle and a crash, and he felt that he had left the room.

Now he was sitting on a train. It was the train that took him from Berlin to Frankfurt, and Anna was sitting by the window when he opened the compartment door. He recognized her instantly.

For a moment he thought about how that could be, and then it occurred to him that the train had departed from East Berlin, where it had picked up a few passengers who were allowed to travel to the West, and they were almost only old people like himself.

He stood outside in the corridor, freezing and waiting while the conductor shoved his suitcase into the luggage rack, and he watched her. Anna had her legs crossed, her small, constantly fluttering hands stroking her knee in a motion that was deeply familiar, moving along the armrests and then reaching her hair. She plucked a strand of hair out and tucked it impatiently behind her ear while she looked outside at the crowded platform, tense and swaying her torso to and fro. It was the strand of hair that made him certain she must have recognized him.

He held onto the sliding door and entered the compartment. There was sunshine inside; he felt dazzled, blinking into the clouds of smoke she blew out; interspersed with light, the smoke framed her face like a grubby curtain.

She said, Hello.

He said, It's you.

The train moved off between the black-framed, permanently dirty, glass roof and walls towards Savignyplatz station.

Age was superimposed upon her body like something not her own, like a cocoon made by time that wasn't really part of her. For a brief moment he had the impression that it was not there for him either, that it was something absolutely unimportant, something transparent that could be wiped away by a single hand.

She rubbed the tips of her shoes together in slight embarrassment and withdrew them beneath her seat.

He hoped she wouldn't ask him anything, anything at all. And they wouldn't want to know anything about one another and wouldn't speak, like they used to, just be together.

She watched him trying to draw the curtain in front of the glass door. In his confusion he pulled it too hard downwards and the brown fabric refused to budge.

That's no use. She laughed aloud.

He sensed his fear, the fear of a fragile man travelling to a place he didn't know.

What can I say . . . he began, tripping over his words, sweating.

They rattled past allotments.

He knew that if other passengers came now he might never be alone with her again, not once.

A suburban train moved alongside them, gradually overtaking. A child, a little girl, pressed her head against the windowpane, breathed on it and wrote something on the fogged glass.

She gave a nervous blink, raised her arms.

Nothing.

No.

It's incredible, isn't it?

Yes, incredible.

He'd met her at the end of the fifties in one of the dance halls on Badstrasse, back when the area close to the border had still been an entertainment district. Anna and he had met up once a week, sometimes twice, in her room near Bornholmer Bridge. He'd never forgotten the look with which she had opened the door to him and said goodbye again a few hours later, a deep, loving look. He had felt it at his back every time he walked down the stairs from her small flat on the third floor, closed the front door behind him and stood outside her building for one last moment beneath the trembling of the railway line, before he went home, only a few hundred yards on the other side of the sector border. That had been during his first marriage.

By the time they reached Wannsee station where the train made its last stop in West Berlin, they were caught up in the efforts of the first sentences. There was an old lady standing on the platform, dressed in a mink coat, in the sunshine. She stood there in high-heeled shoes and swayed, watching the train move past her with no expression on her face. Once he had spotted her he knew instantly that Anna was not old.

He opened his lunch packet rather laboriously, to give himself something to do.

She watched him mockingly as he tried to unwrap his provisions from several layers of grey greaseproof paper.

It's not a good route, she said.

The brakes squealed at Griebnitzsee, just outside of the city.

He felt her drawing back into her seat.

Something military pervaded the carriage, although he had not yet seen any border guards: a dull snappiness. Perhaps because of the way they opened the doors and slammed them shut again, the barking of the dogs.

Are you married?

No.

Cold, bitter-stained air swept along the corridor; he heard calls and the clattering of a two-stroke engine.

Not ever?

No. She pursed her lips.

A pile of rubble was heaped next to the border hut; alongside it an Alsatian, chained to an iron post poking out of the ground at a slant. The dog kept leaping up in wild rage, as far as the chain would allow.

For a long time the train moved at walking pace. He saw an unpaved square, a few sheds, pockmarked houses at the edge of a wood, a village sign: Brück (Mark). He stood up slowly and went over to her. Then they were sitting next to one another, their knees touching from now on every time the train swayed.

The next time they stopped was near Wiesenburg. It must have been raining not long ago, and the train stood motionless on the tracks for twenty minutes alongside a fleet of shovel excavators, giant dinosaurs made of rust, set up in a circle on a grey stretch of wasteland dotted with deep furrows of tyre tracks and shining tongues of puddles in the clay.

Did you stay at the post office all along? she asked.

Yes. What about you?

Sales assistant.

She stretched out her arm and he smelt her perfume, following the hand she stroked across her hair with his eyes.

Between still-bare trees a small decrepit manor house appeared, with dark holes in the places where the tiles had fallen down, beneath them curved roof beams in an onion shape.

He looked at it, she looked away.

Holding hands, they gazed at the Elbe, the river vanishing and reappearing in the distance, vanishing again, and then it grew dark but they didn't turn on any light, still holding one another by the hands without looking at one another.

Building workers perched on tracks in the onsetting darkness. From time to time their yellow lamps flashed, lamps placed on the grey heaps of stones next to the track bed in a dirty tangle of cables and wobbly tripods.

The conductor appeared, inspected their differing tickets and measured the distance between their bodies with a meaningful, pinched look, and then he said, The journey'll take longer today, they're working on the tracks here.

With an effort, he got to his feet and followed the conductor, finding it hard to tear himself away from Anna.

I'm getting off at Bad Hersfeld, she called after him. There were two border guards smoking in the corridor, leaning far out of the window.

. . . next year . . . one of them shouted. He struggled to speak, the airstream crushing his voice.

. . . what?

Supposed to be coming next year.

Yes, but what! What is it?

Just a Trabi.

Hey, what's wrong with a Trabi? A Trabi's good enough!

He reached out his arms, pushing at doors and windows in an attempt to keep his balance on the way to the washroom.

The narrow confines there brought him out in a sweat. He stepped on the pedal on the floor until a thin, brownish stream ran into the basin, dabbed wetness onto his forehead, twisted a crusted black wheel until a few crumbs of soap fell into his hand, and avoided looking at his face—although the mirror took up the whole of the wall above the basin.

He stood there for a long time, waiting for the tears on his face to dry on his skin.

Back in the corridor, his eyes zigzagged between the now partly lit-up compartments and the countryside outside as it grew darker. The land seemed to consist now only of fields, unploughed, with a few straws from the previous year scattered like lines drawn across the ground, and of piles of animal fodder covered with tarpaulins and weighed down with tyres.

An industrial area came over him in the night's haze, a steaming, hissing beast beneath sulphurous lamps, a silvery sprawling growth of tubes and chimneys, on square miles of defoliated, derooted, poison-soaked earth. Very slowly, stammeringly they passed by a steep wall of corrugated iron lined with storage tanks. He stared outside, mesmerized, as a single worker crawled up the high and inconceivably long ladder of a chimney, a dark spot crawling sluggishly onwards, pressed to the chimney's concrete skin, caught in a tunnel of rungs and steel that seemed endless in comparison to the man's size.

He knew he didn't have much time left. When he came back he saw that she had missed him, a trembling, questioning look received him just like back then. But her eyes weren't the same after all, he saw that now, they were coated in something milky that would intensify over the next few years.

Outside, the countryside grew hillier. The last yellow, jagged *W*s of the East German train tracks glided past, open freight cars, tank trains, piles of gravel, the silhouettes of endless plants growing on the embankments. There was nothing they could do but look at one another now, they knew that. They loved one another with their eyes, for a couple of hours, to make up for a life that they had not spent together.

The border guards came and jerked open the door. They seemed to notice there was something in the air that ought to arouse their suspicions, spending minutes reading their passports. He felt his weariness, what great weariness, he hated it, tried to fight it off, saw Anna watching his battle with lenience and slight disappointment, and in the end he did fall asleep.

Was it sleep? A firm, safe state of being, that was how it seemed to him, something he had never had in all the years before or all the months afterwards.

The next thing he saw was a village in the middle of West Germany. He stared in bewilderment at the picket fences, the wide, brightly lit terraces of the small houses, their new-fangled, homely ugliness. The seat next to his was empty, only a small piece of squared paper left on it. And the border guards had vanished, all of it gone, like a dream.

Keep on, he thought. Don't stop now. He dragged himself forwards, reaching a perfectly normal basement partition a few steps on. A strange coldness hung about the room, damper than in the cold-storage room, more penetrating. He shivered.

This is *his* cellar, he thought. Then it's mine too. He felt the wish to stay here. It was so strong it scared him.

He looked at the fragile lines left behind on the dusty floor by a broom, then at the trunk there. A not particularly large trunk, standing in the room like a foreign body, making it look even emptier. He shook his head at himself. He'd been in the house for months and never come down here. Here, where there seemed to be answers to his questions.

He placed his hand on the lid, looked for and found a name: large, slightly clumsy white letters that entrenched themselves in his head, disintegrating into lines, swirling round and coming together again.

Could he open it, this trunk? He squatted slightly and felt at its edge; there was just a simple bolt. He pushed it aside, leant over and lifted the lid. It slid silently upward.

Clothes, folded up; he couldn't make out much else. A flat, cold shaft of light pushed its way into the room through the basement window from a small lamp by the shed that was always alight in the backyard.

Parts of a uniform: a grey military blouse. He felt his way across the woollen cloth, the wide front pockets, a scarf and something rougher, also made of cloth, with buckles. He pulled it out: a pair of gaiters. Inside the gaiters was a small case. He opened it. Something greenish-brown, folded, was inside it; he spread it out, held it up to the weak light: a gas cape.

A ration bag—he opened it; it was empty. What a familiar action that had once been, opening a canvas ration bag more than thirty years ago, a single hand movement with the power to render all the time passed meaningless for a moment.

Cardboard boxes holding old shoes, a silver picture frame, tarnished but bereft of any photos, records, brushes, a barometer. Between them a bundle tied up with string. He plucked at the string in vain, eventually biting it open with his teeth.

A sheet of paper fell towards him: a letter from a missing persons tracing office. He knew the letter; a copy of it had been among the papers of the will. And he had read it over and over, he knew every sentence off by heart.

With reference to information provided by other persons, it had said, and on the basis of returnee reports, descriptions of combat operations, War diaries and army and specialist maps, it can be assumed that the aforementioned individual is highly likely to have fallen in action.

He brooded, as he had so often. Was there some kind of hint hidden in these lines that might bring him clarity?

He came upon a pile of photos, picked them up and pressed them to his chest but they slipped out of his fingers — all except one, which his hands just managed to grip. He held it towards the window.

Men in the snow, at the rear of an army truck, smoking. Behind them a very large village sign, obviously in Poland or on the border to Poland. They were stuck on a country lane and the truck had a flat tyre; one of the men was holding a jack up to the camera and grinning. A large canvas partly concealed the interior of the truck, from behind it a pile of long, grey objects peeped out, perhaps metal pipes or rifle barrels. Everything in the photo was in sharp focus, making it strangely scaled down, the even focus blending out the difference between the foreground and the background.

Was Müller there, was he one of them?

He remembered a Müller, a man with a broken leg whom he'd helped out of a drainage ditch and then pushed a little way on a handbarrow — could it be him, one of these men?

He didn't know.

Then there was another Müller, who had kept coming to mind; he'd built bunkers with him. That Müller had had a frostbitten ear that got infected, his ear had swollen up like a balloon. He had punctured it with a needle, and that Müller had said, I'll be grateful to you for ever; perhaps it was him in the picture?

Had he met this Müller as a dying man or beforehand, when he had still been healthy?

He knew whenever he thought about all this for too long he felt dragged into a dark tunnel, in which everything was shapeless and formless, but that was just evading the issue. Something he had simply been putting forward as a pretext for years.

He had tried to think of all the dead he remembered from the War but there were too many. And nor was it possible to remember only the dead German soldiers.

The more he tried, the more clearly the many other dead came to the fore, all the dead from his brief involvement in the first weeks of the invasion of the Soviet Union and all the countless dead during his time in the guard detail of a transit camp the following winter, in Poland.

It was the prisoners from the camp especially that had dogged him since then, countless starving men. They still had no accommodation by the time it got cold, walking through the snow with feverish faces, endlessly up and down and up and down, so as not to freeze to death, and some nights now he was tortured by the thought of

what it was like to see the world through the last gaze of
their eyes; the other exhausted men, the dead men, the
men guarding them, the accurately quadratic barbed
wire, put up by himself and others very carefully and
calmly over several days, reinforced with wooden posts,
provided with raised lookouts for better observation, the
edge of the woods, the administration huts, the watch-
towers, the way all that swayed before their eyes and
they had to keep moving, walking, walking, on and on,
walking until it was all over at last.

The sameness of the fear-ridden time after he received the letter informing him of the inheritance had made
it shrink to a short phase of dull days in his memory but
it had really been not days but months, in which he had
sat at home and hardly eaten and drunk little and moved
even less, a long time during which he had finally come
to understand his guilt, a huge, cold, black shadow
across him.

He looked at the photo again, more carefully now.

There was another path turning off from the road
behind the truck, bordering on a field, a grey, branching
track between snow-capped furrows. Behind it the level
ground fell away into a kind of depression, with dark
surfaces, darker than the snow and the white of the sky:
the roofs of a village, a station.

The picture seemed to absorb him now — he saw
himself hurrying along the path, at his back the men's
laughter, the sound of the truck. Ahead of him the blond

man with the soot on his jacket, looking round hastily
from time to time; he had soot on his arms as well and he
swiped an arm across his face as he ran on, soot and fear
resting on his forehead like a dark weight.

He saw the assembly point, a provisionally sectioned-
off area behind the station where five hundred men had
been corralled together for several weeks; he saw the
guard at the gate, he said to him, A Russian, just one man,
what do you want with him? There'll be a thousand of
them by tomorrow and five thousand the day after that;
he saw the guards on duty, housed in a decommissioned
railway carriage, their heads, outlines of bottles,
cigarettes in the corners of their mouths, rifle barrels,
expressions dulled by stupor, leaning bored out of the
broken windows of open train compartments, and then he
saw the prisoners, so many of them, the dead lying on the
ground between them.

He tore himself free, slipping into a kind of darkness.

There was the corridor again, a clay corridor, no
proper floor. It was damp and musty here. And he had
to get to the door, to that door.

He felt his thoughts revolving ever faster as he kept
moving forward.

The stranger's arrival time occurred to him; that must
be important. And what about the flowers, the bouquet
the boy had held in his hand? They hadn't been wilted —
pansies from the flowerpot in the backyard — even though

the butcher's wife watered them so erratically; the flowers usually bowed their heads early in the morning, unless they had shade because someone had parked in front of them, in the parking space for hotel guests.

The stranger's car must have been there, right by the flowers, at least when he'd left the house in the afternoon, and later, early in the evening when he came home, he had seen it.

Why had he not noticed the car in the morning; how could that be? If it had been there in the morning he ought to have seen it.

And was the stranger one of the men on the wanted poster at all? A woman in the bottom right-hand corner, the man had said on the telephone. But there hadn't been a woman.

The second poster ought to have been on the advertising pillar, he had seen one there the day before — but what poster? The same as the one in the butcher's window or a different one? And the man with the paste brush, he'd had a large sheet of paper with him, had turned to the pillar, looked round furtively. Hadn't there been children's hands on it? Yes, children's hands, red prints in the shape of children's hands.

He struggled for air.

He tried to understand what was happening but it made no sense. It set in, proceeded, broke off — making no sense. You came into the world and lived your life but you didn't feel time passing; and then your life came to an end and you had to accept that you understood nothing at all, not even the simplest of things did you understand.

He staggered further onward.

Cold, wet. Wood.

And there was something else, something he smelt: blood, already stale, or offal. A weak but clear trace.

He reached the door. It seemed unimportant to him now, just a wooden door knocked together out of a few nails and boards. It closed in an alcove in the wall. On the other side of it was the white plastic trough, empty, obviously hastily shoved in there, its lid slipped aside. And behind it, weakly lit from inside, a cabinet with a glass door, standing like a shrine on a brick pedestal, emitting a hum.

Part of the glass was misted over; he could make out the shape of a skinned animal's head and other cuts of meat: ribs, trotters, limbs; a stamp of the word *Freibank* on a rind of fat identified it as low quality, slaughter-house by-product.

He fell to his knees and vomited.

A rounded, glinting hog's head. The longer he looked at it, the more it seemed to be shifting, changing colour and lengthening, looking like the head of a horse. And the smells intensified, now it smelt of alcohol, per-spiration, rotten meat. He saw a group of men on a dusty road, moving towards a large space: soldiers, drunks. He heard an ugly jeering: Feeding time — his own voice melting into the others — Feeding time at the zoo. The horse had been dead a long time. They dragged it to the fence on a rope. Its belly was bloated and strewn with black spots, a piece of meat had been cut out of the rear with a knife, the end of its spine poked out, scratching lines on the sandy ground. He stared at it now, straining as if to decipher a message in a foreign language. A motion caught hold of the crowd behind the fence. Some of them, those who could still move quickly, rushed to a certain place that they seemed to make out in advance, and the others, the weaker ones, followed them slowly, all moving towards the animal like a single body, a huge, many-armed and many-legged creature.

Someone threw a lit cigarette into the fenced-off area. He looked at the hand that had held it: his own. One of the prisoners leapt upon it, and another threw the first man to the ground and tried to get it out of his clutches. And then he saw the horse again, now lying on a slightly sloping piece of ground, and they let go of it and kicked it until it rolled to the fence, and a man standing at the very front caught hold of one hoof and pulled at it, mustered all his strength to pull it closer, ramming his teeth into a stretch of hide; others launched themselves at him, crushing him, he tore his mouth open, and he couldn't stop looking, there it was again, that opening, the never-ending hole behind the things, the dizzying depth behind that agonized, dying mouth that he had never forgotten.

The old man was waving his arms now crazily, beating about himself as if to scare something off. But he knew that was no longer possible, he was there now where his end had always been awaiting him, with the images that had shifted slowly, over decades, to the centre of his being.

He fell backwards, hitting the back of his head on something, groaning. Something for which he had no name grabbed at the back of his neck. It seemed to be further behind him; he didn't know whether merely beyond his field of vision or entirely beyond his perception.

His body moved now without his volition. It scraped along the ground, down the corridor, into another room where two heaps of coal were piled up, it was lifted up and placed gently at the top of one of the heaps.

He looked around.

He gasped for breath, felt the pressure of the air that he drew in with a hiss, in bursts, felt the dryness of his mouth.

The questions hammered in his head. What was this house here? Why had he inherited it, just like that, undeservedly, from a man he didn't even know? Because he had helped someone out of a ditch, was that why? Because he had held a needle to an infected ear, because of such petty things?

A man shuffled in. He looked weak. He clambered onto the second, slightly lower coal heap, sat down, took a long, sad look at him and tried to drink from a tin cup riddled with holes. A piece of wood with a number written on it hung from a string round his neck and the water escaped in all directions from the holes in the cup; he put a desperate hand underneath it and held it open for a moment and then watched the water flowing to the floor through the gaps between his fingers.

The old man tried to get upright, screwing up his eyes to focus on the figure.

Was it him, the man from the village who he thought he had recognized months later and many miles to the west, the spectrally thin man caught on the fence?

He knew there were no more answers, only questions.

The scrap of paper fell out of his pocket as he propped himself up on the coal to change his position. A short, hard shock shook his body. Only a moment later did he realize it was happiness.

He'd had it on him all along, and something inside him had known it was that way. Her name was written on the scrap of paper and an address, he was quite sure of that. And the street name was underlined twice, if he remembered rightly.

His hand trembled as he screwed up the paper, enclosing it in his fist, and then he unclenched it again, saw the paper slipping slowly down the brittle, black boulders, into a tiny crack that had opened up between the lumps, and all that was left was a pile of coal, dark, dirty and glittering.

Panic descended on him, he began scrabbling, digging his hands into the black depths, frantic, caught hold of something and drew it up. Was it his paper?

Yes, it felt like paper and he was so happy. It shone weakly in the darkness, was paler than the damp walls with their covering of cobwebs, the crumbling, indefinable floor of the cellar, the whole grey emptiness of this endless night.

He felt he had the wish to unfold and read what he had in his hand—just one last time.

Through a kind of fog, he saw a third Müller, a very young man, lying on a stretcher at a level crossing.

And he heard voices.

He knew one of them was his own voice.

Tell me your name. There was no reply.

Tell me where you're from.

Had he answered? He couldn't make out the answer.

Have you got something to write with?

Yes.

Can you post a letter for me?

Perhaps.

It's almost finished.

I don't know.

To my family.

I don't know.

They won't even know I'm dying.

In the final hours, he had always thought, the most important moments of your life pass you by, and you could take a look at them in peace—they had no meaning any more.

He had been married twice and gone on a few vacations, to Venice, to Capri, to Austria, to Ireland. In the fifties, he had survived a fall from some scaffolding he had climbed up on, just for a laugh, drunk. He had played cards. He had spent thousands of days standing behind a post-office counter.

He lay still and waited for something else to come but nothing happened.

Dawn came. Cautiously, he raised his head, noting the light that now cast its echo everywhere outside, on the base of the building opposite, on a pile of greengrocer's crates with a couple of leftover stalks between scraps of paper, on bicycles, bottles, sawn-off pieces of wood and parts of a car's bodywork that reflected something for him, perhaps the sky.

And then came the light.

It came much faster than he had thought; it filled the room, crept into all things as a dazzling brightness and carried him away.

His hands slipped slightly across his body, the fabric in which he was swathed. He felt his hands on the cool of the sheet and clenched his fists.

And he struggled. His breaths now came like pull-ups. Too confined, too hard was this body to let much more inside it; his time, almost run out. He felt that. And he felt himself grow sad, amid all his efforts, which he didn't give up after all.